BRANDON BRUSACH

Dícheall

First published by Brusach Books 2026

First edition

ISBN: 9798998671340

This book was professionally typeset on Reedsy.
Find out more at reedsy.com

Contents

Foreword

As a person blessed with Irish ancestry, I have always been drawn to the study of Irish culture, traditions, language, and history. This inclination fostered in me a deep appreciation for Irish music, which I have enjoyed for many years now. During my university studies, I took a course titled *Ireland and the Irish* that helped me to gain a more comprehensive understanding of Irish history and society, as well as their long struggle for freedom and sovereignty. It was during that course that I came to learn about a fascinating organization called *The Fenian Brotherhood.* This was something like a secret society, set up by Irish-American immigrants, many of whom would go on to serve in the US Civil War. Their ultimate goal was to free the nation of Ireland from the foreign domination imposed upon them at the hands of the British. To accomplish this, the Fenians would wage an armed struggle in North America, launching multiple raids into British Canada. Whilst conducting my research, I was surprised to learn that this story is greatly underrepresented in the historical record. To my knowledge, it only appears in a handful of nonfiction books. It is my hope that *Dícheall* will fill a literary gap and shine light on this unique period in history. Perhaps, if we are so fortunate, it may even been made into a feature length film or perhaps a mini-series. We shall see.

1

Cairdeas Gaoil - Kinsmen

The war was over, and the city had gone mad with joy.

Seamus heard it before he saw it. The bells, the cheering, the distant crack of celebratory gunfire somewhere uptown. New York had swallowed the news of the Union victory and was drunk on it, every street corner a festival, every window a stage. Women leaned from tenement frames and threw flowers down onto the procession. Children ran alongside the column of blue-coated men, grabbing at their sleeves.

Seamus kept his eyes forward. His uniform hung off him like clothes left on a scarecrow. The jacket threadbare at the elbows, the trousers pale and thinned at the knees from long marches through mud he'd sooner forget. The scar along his jaw caught the afternoon light.

"Would ye look at this." Rónán walked beside him, grinning wide enough to split his face. He spread his arms as a fistful of flower petals rained down from above. "The city has finally found love for us. All it cost us was four years of misery."

"You've a gift for philosophy."

"Cork men always do."

They were moving through the Five Points now, the streets narrower, the buildings pressing close on both sides. The crowd here was different. A bit rougher, louder, more familiar. Irish faces everywhere. Women with shawls, old men in flat caps, barefoot children dodging between the legs of adults. Someone had strung a green banner across the mouth of an alley. The banner read *Éirinn go Brách* in gold lettering. The smell of boiled cabbage and coal smoke mixed with something sweeter that drifted out from every propped-open doorway.

A broad man with a red face and enormous white mutton chops stepped directly into their path, blocking them as though they were cattle he intended to redirect.

"You lads Irish Brigade?"

"69th Infantry." Rónán tapped the badge on his coat.

The man's face broke open. He put an arm around Rónán. "Saints be praised. Welcome home boys." He turned to Seamus and pumped his hand with both of his own, a grip like a vice. "Michael Conroy. This is my pub." He jerked his thumb toward a narrow doorway painted green, a hand-lettered sign above it that read *Conroy's*. "The pair of ye are coming inside. I'll not hear otherwise."

Rónán looked at Seamus. Seamus looked at the door. They went inside.

The place was already heaving. Men stood shoulder to shoulder at the bar, spilling out between tables where soldiers and civilians sat tangled together, arms around each other's necks, some with tears still drying on their cheeks, some with mouths open in song. A fiddler in the far corner sawed through a reel, competing with the voices around him and losing cheerfully.

The barman was a young lad, thin, with ink-dark hair. He

spotted their uniforms and leaned across the bar.

"Veterans drink free tonight." He set two glasses down and filled them without being asked.

Rónán lifted his glass immediately. "To the fighting Irish!"

Seamus wrapped his fingers around the glass. The whiskey was rough and warm and he let it sit for a moment, watching the room. An old man at the next table wept quietly while a soldier, his son from the look of it, gripped his hand across the wood. Three men near the window were bellowing out *The Bold Fenian Men*, off-key and without apology. Somebody stood on a chair and proposed a toast to the dead of Fredericksburg and the room went briefly, reverently quiet before erupting again.

Seamus and Rónán paid respects to their fallen comrades, telling their stories alongside all the others. The 69th New York Infantry had fought at Antietam where they defeated the famed Confederate Brigade, the Louisiana Tigers. They fought at Fredericksburg, Chancellorsville, Gettysburg, and were present for the surrender at Appomattox.

Rónán raised his glass. "To life and liberty."

Seamus drank.

The second round arrived without anyone asking for it.

A man set the pints down on the table, tall straight-sided pewter tankards filled to the top with a perfect head of foam. The man then pulled up a stool as though he'd been expected. He was perhaps forty, broad through the chest, with a close-trimmed dark beard shot through with silver and eyes that moved quickly around the room before settling. He dressed better than most in the pub. A wool coat with brass buttons. A hat he removed and placed on his knee.

"You lads 69th?"

"What gave it away." Seamus plucked at his jacket lapel.

The man smiled. "I've bought a lot of drinks tonight. Not for every soldier. Just for the Irish ones." He extended a hand. "Ciarán Flood."

Seamus shook it. The grip was firm, deliberate.

Flood leaned forward on his elbows, dropped his voice beneath the noise of the pub. The fiddler had started up again, which helped.

"Brothers, I won't waste your time. I'm here to talk about the occupation. British boots remain on Irish soil. They trample and oppress our people, just as they have for centuries. But we continue to resist British tyranny, even in exile. There are men in this city who are organizing to secure the future of the Irish nation."

Rónán set his pint down. "Doing what, exactly?"

Flood reached inside his coat and produced a folded pamphlet, which he slid across the table to Seamus. "Read that first. Then I'll talk."

Seamus unfolded it. The paper was thick, good quality, and the front bore an intricate knotwork border, the interlocking lines of it dense and deliberate, framing a harp at the center with a sunburst behind it. Rónán leaned across his shoulder.

The slogans ran in bold type between illustrations of men at arms, of a green coastline, of a broken chain.

Ireland Unfettered. Ireland Unbroken.

Below that, a longer declaration, dense with the language of martyrdom and destiny. Seamus turned the page. More patriotic artwork. A map of Ireland with its provinces named. A list of grievances against the Crown going back centuries.

Near the bottom, a single line in larger type than the rest.

Seamus read it aloud. *"The Irish do not forget! Fight for an Irish*

Republic!"

The table was quiet for a moment.

"We are the Fenian Brotherhood." Flood folded his hands. "We've been building for years. Men from every ward in this city. Alongside our brothers in Boston, Philadelphia, and Chicago. Veterans like yourselves, men who know how to march and how to fight, men who didn't spend four years learning that skill just to go back to digging ditches."

"You're talking about armed struggle." Seamus kept his voice low.

"I'm talking about taking action. Coordinated, organized, serious action." Flood's eyes moved to him. "The Brits don't fear petitions. They don't fear speeches. The only thing they've ever respected is force."

Seamus turned the pamphlet over in his hands.

"There are meetings." Flood looked between the two of them. "Every Tuesday. Croton Hall, down on Mulberry. Come once, listen, learn what we're about. That's all I'm asking."

Rónán scratched his jaw. "And if we don't like what we hear?"

"Then you walk out and I never bother you again."

Seamus set the pamphlet flat on the table. He thought about Mayo. Not a memory exactly, more a sensation, the Atlantic smell of it, the cold, the dark cone of the Reek against a grey sky, things he'd carried since childhood the way a man carries a stone in his boot. He thought about his aunt standing on the dock, not weeping, which had frightened him more than tears would have. He had not seen the Emerald Isle since he was a young boy.

Flood picked up his hat. "Ireland is full of people who wish things were different. She needs men who'll make them different." He looked at Seamus squarely. "Able-bodied men capable of what is called for. The future of the Irish people is sitting at tables exactly like this one."

He stood, nodded once, and moved back into the crowd.

Rónán picked up the pamphlet. Stared at the harp.

"Should we join?" he asked.

Seamus took a long pull of his pint. Lacking a reason to say otherwise, he shrugged his shoulders and agreed to attend a single meeting of the Fenian Brotherhood, to get their measure and see what could be done to help the Irish back home across the Atlantic.

2

Mionn - The Oath

The chapel held perhaps forty people, packed onto wooden pews. A few half-melted candles sat on the altar, their light warm and unsteady. The smell was tallow and damp wool and the faint sweetness of incense that had soaked into the stone over decades.

Father Declan stood at the front with a Bible open in his hands. He was a broad man, somewhere in his mid-fifties, with iron-grey hair cropped close and a face shaped by sagging cheeks and bushy eyebrows. He wore his collar and read without preamble.

"It is easy for many to be overcome by few; and in the sight of God there is no difference between deliverance by many or by few. For victory in war does not depend on the size of the army, but on the strength that comes from heaven."

The room was still. Seamus sat with his hands on his knees, his eyes on the priest. Seamus and Rónán had been attending the meetings of the Fenian Brotherhood and steadily involving themselves in the organization's political activities. It was through the Brotherhood that Seamus came to know Father Declan, who provided the secret society with its spiritual backbone.

"First Maccabees." Declan closed the Bible and set it on the table. "Some of you will know the Maccabees. Most of you, I'd wager, do not." He moved to stand in front of the table. "They were Jewish rebels. Freedom fighters. Their homeland had been taken by a foreign empire, their people subjugated, their culture outlawed, their temple desecrated. And they were outnumbered. Always outnumbered."

He let that sit for a moment.

"And yet they fought. Judas Maccabeus took to the hills with a small band of men, and he struck at a force vastly superior in arms and numbers. And he prevailed! Not because God loves violence. But because God lends strength to men who fight for what is right and just."

Rónán leaned close to Seamus's ear. "He's talking about us."

"I know," Seamus whispered.

Declan's eyes moved across the room. "The British Empire is large. It is powerful. It has the largest navy in the world, old institutions, more soldiers than you can count. And every man in this room knows what that empire has done to Ireland. You've lived it. Your fathers lived it. Your fathers' fathers." His voice didn't rise. It didn't need to. "They took our land off us and let our people starve while they grew fat off the rent. They banned our language. They taxed our existence. And when we could no longer pay, they watched us board coffin ships and scatter to the four winds."

A man two rows ahead of Seamus had his jaw set hard and his eyes fixed somewhere beyond the wall.

"But the Maccabees teach us something essential." Declan picked up the Bible again, not to read from it, just to hold. "That the measure of empire is not the measure of God. That ten thousand spears do not guarantee victory. That a small people, righteous in their cause, have reclaimed their homeland before." He looked at the room. "And they can do so again."

Seamus exhaled slowly through his nose. He'd heard patriotic speeches before, in pubs, in halls, standing in the street while men climbed on crates and hollered. This was different. The Word of God carried a different weight than any pamphlet or recruiting broadside. It settled into him somewhere deeper than argument could reach.

After, when the men dispersed in twos and threes into the dark street, Seamus and Rónán remained behind, discussing their recent activities with the Brotherhood and their desire to deepen their commitment. Declan gathered his Bible and was preparing to leave when he noticed the young men still in the pew.

"The passage reached you."

"It did, Father." Seamus turned his cap in his hands. "I believe now we can finally see the path forward."

"We're ready to take the oath," Rónán added.

Father Declan raised his bushy eyebrows. "Are you certain?"

"We are!" Seamus confirmed.

The three men gathered before the altar. Father Declan laid his Bible down before them.

"Place your right hand upon the Book. State your name when I pause. Then repeat the words after me, phrase by phrase. There is no shame in going slowly. These words will be with you the rest of your life."

Seamus did as he was told. With solemnity and purpose, he swore an oath before God.

"I, Seamus McKenna, do solemnly swear, in the presence of Almighty God, that I will do my utmost, at every risk, while life lasts, to make Ireland a free and independent Republic.

That I will yield obedience, in all things not contrary to the law of God, to the lawful commands of my superior officers in the Brotherhood.

That I will labor without ceasing, in whatever capacity I am called, to establish and defend a Republican government in Ireland by whatever means the cause shall require of me.

That I will foster among my brothers a spirit of unity, of nationality, and of love for our people, at home and in exile, and will not allow that spirit to be broken by threat, by hardship, or by despair.

That I will preserve inviolable secrecy regarding all transactions of this Brotherhood confided to me, revealing nothing to any person not entitled to know it, under any circumstance, by any compulsion.

That I do not now belong to any society antagonistic to this Brotherhood, and will not join such a society while I remain a member of it.

That I take this obligation freely, without reservation or evasion, knowing that any violation merits the severest judgment of my brothers and of the Almighty.

I will endeavor to free Ireland. So help me God."

As they finished the oath, Seamus and Rónán bent forward and gently kissed the Bible. Father Declan embraced the new members and showered them with love and praise. Seamus and Rónán stepped into their new status and responsibility, emboldened and confident, ready for any task the Brotherhood might assign them.

3

Greim agus Fuil - Glue and Blood

The city was a different place altogether before dawn. The streets belonged to cart horses and rats and men who didn't want to be seen, and the three of them suited the hour well enough.

Seamus carried the bucket. Rónán carried the roll of broadsides under one arm, the brush in his free hand. They moved in silence down Mulberry Street, picking their spots, the blank side of a building where a shopfront met bare brick, the flat face of a fence post, the boarded window of a shuttered tailor's. Seamus would slap the wheat paste on thick and fast and Rónán would press the broadside flat, smoothing from the center outward with his palms, working out the bubbles.

The designs were the work of Finn Ó Treasaigh. Seamus had met the man only briefly and learned that he was some sort of creative. He was a writer, a poet, and he could also draw. The Brotherhood had tapped him to create a series of recruitment posters, among other useful materials. The one currently being distributed depicted the Emerald Isle and a heroic Gael rescuing a goddess-like woman from bondage. The text read *IRELAND*

WILL BE FREE! Below it, in smaller text, the meeting times and location could be found.

They had pasted perhaps a dozen by the time they turned onto a narrower side street, the buildings pressing closer, the sky above them just beginning to separate from black into deep blue. Rónán stopped walking.

"Would ye look at that."

Above the door of a small hardware merchant, nailed directly to the lintel, a hand-painted sign. The letters were neat, deliberate, the work of someone who had taken their time.

HELP WANTED. NO BLACKS. NO MEXICANS. NO IRISH.

Seamus read it twice. He wasn't sure why he read it twice. The words didn't change.

"Right there in the open." Rónán stood with the roll of broadsides tucked under his arm, his head tilted back. "Doesn't even bother to whisper it."

"Never did." Seamus set the bucket down. The paste steamed faintly in the cold air. "I had a foreman on the docks when I was fourteen. Posted it on a board outside the site office. *No Irish.* Clear as anything. Took it down after a week because enough of us showed up anyway and he needed the labor."

"Because the work was brutal and no one else would do it."

Seamus picked the bucket back up. "How many thousands of Irish came over to fight in the war? Boys of seventeen who'd never held a rifle before they enlisted." He looked at the sign again. "Years of service to this nation and their brothers can't get hired to sweep a floor."

Rónán shook his head slowly. "We fight and bleed for her and America still won't have us at the table."

"No respect to be found. A real shame."

Rónán was quiet for a moment. Then he peeled one broadside

from the roll, an older design from the previous year. He dipped the brush into the bucket and coated the wall directly beside the merchant's door with a long, generous stroke of paste.

Seamus pressed the broadside flat.

The sunburst harp blazed up out of the dark brick, crisp and defiant, *IRISH AND PROUD* sitting not two feet from the merchant's neat little sign.

Rónán stepped back and examined the effect. "An improvement to the neighborhood, I'd say."

Seamus picked up the bucket and they walked on.

Since joining the Brotherhood, Seamus and Rónán had taken on a number of minor tasks for the organization. They helped drive turnout to meetings and brought new members into the fold. Additionally, they helped to sell official Fenian Bonds, raising significant sums of money to eventually be paid back by the Irish Republic the Brotherhood intended to birth.

The junction at Baxter and Worth was empty at this hour, just a gas lamp guttering above the intersection and the dark mouths of alleys on three sides. Seamus began to apply the wheat paste to a fresh spot. Rónán was unrolling the next broadside when a man stepped out of a doorway across the street.

He was heavy through the middle, wool coat, a docker's cap pulled low. He looked at the bucket, at the broadsides, at the freshly pasted wall behind them.

"The hell are you Paddy bastards doing to this street?"

Seamus straightened. Rónán didn't look up from the roll.

"Decorating." Rónán pulled a broadside free.

The man crossed toward them, his boots loud on the cobbles. "Mick rubbish, that's what that is." He jabbed a finger at the nearest poster. "Criminal filth pasted all over decent people's neighborhood. You Fenian bog-trotters think this is your city?"

"We live here same as you," Seamus said.

"Your lot shouldn't be anywhere near here," He'd stopped a few feet short, close enough for Seamus to smell the beer on him. He turned his head and bellowed back toward the doorway he'd come from. "Oi — come out here."

Three men emerged. Younger, two of them, moving with the loose energy of men who'd been waiting for something to happen. The third was broader, darker, Italian by his looks, with a flat, patient face and his hands already loose at his sides.

"Fenian crooks out posting their propaganda." The first man spoke to his friends without looking away from Seamus.

"We're going." Seamus reached for the bucket handle.

One of the younger men stepped past Rónán and snatched the roll of broadsides from under his arm. He held it up, grinning, then gripped both ends and tore it down the middle with a wet ripping sound, scattering paper across the cobbles.

Rónán hit him.

It was a short, direct punch, no windup, and the young man went back two steps. Then it was everywhere at once. Fisticuffs. The first man lunged for Rónán and the other young one threw himself at Seamus, but the Italian got there first, a straight right hand that Seamus had no time to read.

The fist caught him across the bridge of the nose. His eyes filled with water and white light and he felt the warm rush of blood over his upper lip, tasted iron. He blinked hard and threw himself to the right, putting distance between them, getting his hands up.

The Italian man came forward methodically. Seamus harried his advance with jabs, keeping him at bay. His opponent stood toe to toe with him, landing his own quick, stinging blows. A wad of knuckles popped Seamus on the nose again, inflaming it further. Seamus caught the next punch on his forearm and stepped inside, then drove a left hook hard into the man's ribs. The Italian man folded around it, his breath coming out in one short bark, both arms dropping to protect his body. Seamus felt the impact travel up through his wrist and into his shoulder.

The man crumpled sideways against the wall and stayed there.

He turned.

Rónán had the first man's coat in his fist and was taking punishment from the other two, who had pulled him off their friend. Outnumbered, the Irishman struggled to defend himself against their assault.

Rónán reached into his coat.

The long knife came out in a single motion. The Bowie pattern, heavy-spined blade caught what little light the gas lamp threw. He slashed sideways across the man in front of him, a fast backhand arc, and the man lurched away with a hiss of breath, one forearm clutched to his chest where a thin line of dark opened across his sleeve. The one holding Rónán released him immediately and both men backed away, hands up, eyes fixed on the blade.

"Irish thugs! *Hooligans!*" one of the assailants spat. "They mean to murder us!"

The whistle split the pre-dawn quiet like a crack of glass.

Seamus spun. An NYPD police officer was running hard from the far end of Baxter Street, his baton already out, his cape flaring behind him. The man was thirty yards off and closing fast, and somewhere behind him, further back in the dark, came the answering shriek of a second whistle, then a third.

"Run." Seamus grabbed Rónán by the collar.

They fled.

The bucket hit the cobbles and spilled wheat paste in a long white arc across the street. The knife went back inside Rónán's coat without thought, and then they were moving, boots loud and graceless on the stone, ducking left off Baxter onto a narrow cut between two tenements that barely qualified as a street.

Behind them the officer shouted. *Stop! Stop in the name of the law!*

Seamus didn't look back. His nose was still bleeding freely and the blood ran into his mouth, metallic and warm. He spat and ran harder. Rónán was a half-step ahead of him, his long legs eating up the ground, his coat streaming behind him.

The alley opened onto another street, wider, with a cart parked against one kerb and a sleeping horse attached to it. They crossed at a diagonal and plunged into the gap between a laundry and a cobbler's, the walls so close Seamus's shoulders brushed both sides. The smell of lye soap hit him sharp and chemical. His boot came down in something soft and wet and he didn't look at what it was.

The gap let them out into a small yard, a wooden fence on the far side, perhaps five feet high.

Rónán went over it without slowing, grabbed the top plank, swung his legs up and dropped. Seamus followed a beat behind, his palms catching rough wood, a splinter driving into the meat below his thumb. He landed badly on the far side, his left ankle turning on uneven ground, pain flaring bright up his shin, and he stumbled three steps before Rónán's hand found his arm and steadied him.

They pressed against the fence, breathing hard, and listened.

Boots on cobblestones. Two men, maybe three, passing the far end of the alley they'd come through. A voice, low and clipped. The whistle again, closer, then receding. Then nothing but the distant rumble of an early cart somewhere uptown and his own pulse loud in his ears.

Rónán had his back flat to the fence, his chest heaving. He turned his head and looked at Seamus. His left eye was beginning to swell, the skin below it already darkening toward purple.

"Your eye," Seamus said quietly.

"Your nose." Rónán touched his own face with two fingers and winced. "We match."

Seamus pressed his sleeve against his upper lip. The bleeding had slowed but the front of his shirt was ruined. He breathed through his mouth and checked the yard around them. A small dead garden, a rusted iron pump, the back wall of a boarding house with one window lit on the upper floor, curtains drawn.

He looked at his hands. The wheat paste had dried in the creases of his palms, white and cracked, and the splinter from the fence sat just under the skin at the base of his thumb, a dark sliver.

All around them, the city was humming again, indifferent, resuming its slow business of becoming morning.

Rónán had a suggestion.

"Nóra's," he said, still breathing through his mouth. "She'll sort us."

Seamus nodded. His ankle throbbed steadily with each step and his nose had stopped bleeding properly but sat swollen and tender across the bridge, the skin tight. He tested the ankle's weight, found it tolerable, and followed Rónán out of the yard and onto the street beyond.

Mulberry Street was beginning to wake. A baker's boy trundled past with a flat board of loaves balanced on his head, paying them no mind. A woman shook a rug from a second-floor window, dust and crumbs falling in the grey light. Neither Seamus nor Rónán spoke on the walk over.

Nóra Flannery answered the door before Rónán had finished knocking.

She looked at them with the instinctual concern of a mother. Her grey hair was pinned up hastily, and she wore an apron over her day clothes, a wooden spoon still in her hand.

"Inside." She stood back from the door. "Both of ye."

The kitchen was warm, the stove already lit, a pot of something sitting on it. She set the spoon down and pulled a chair away from the table with her foot, then pointed at it.

"Sit." To Rónán: "You too. There."

Seamus sat. The warmth of the room hit him all at once, the kind that made the cold he'd been carrying in his bones announce itself properly. He set his elbows on the table and pressed his fingers against the bridge of his nose and breathed.

Nóra had a tin box open on the counter. She worked without asking what had happened, which told him she already had a reasonable guess. A cloth came out, then a brown bottle, then a small curved needle threaded with something dark.

She stood in front of Seamus first, tilted his chin up with two fingers, and studied his nose. Her hands were broad and calloused, the hands of someone who had spent many years wringing out laundry.

"Not broken." She pressed either side of the bridge and he flinched. "Probably."

"That's reassuring."

"Hush." She soaked the cloth and pressed it to his upper lip. The sting was sharp and clean, carbolic, and he gripped the edge of the table until it passed. She worked efficiently, no ceremony, cleaning the blood from his face and inspecting the splinter in his palm. A needle and a steady hand dealt with that in thirty seconds. She wrapped his hand with a strip of linen.

Rónán got the same treatment across the table. His eye had swelled considerably, the socket half-closed, the skin beneath it a deep red edging toward black. Nóra pressed a folded cloth soaked in cold water against it and told him to hold it there.

"Who started it?" she said, moving back to the stove.

"They did," Rónán offered.

"Technically," Seamus added.

Nóra set two bowls on the table. Porridge, thick and salted, with a heel of bread beside each. She poured tea from a pot that had been sitting on the back of the stove, already stewed dark, and placed the cups down without asking whether they wanted any.

Seamus wrapped both hands around his cup. The heat moved through the linen wrapping and into his palm. He looked at the bowl, at the bread, at the cup, and something in his chest loosened in a way he hadn't anticipated and couldn't fully account for.

He ate.

Nóra sat across from them with her own cup, watching them eat. She asked no further questions. When Rónán's bowl was empty she refilled it without being asked.

Seamus thought of the parents he'd lost long ago. Had his mother been around, she would've patched him up and fed him the way Nóra had. There was simply the warmth and the food and a woman who had opened the door without hesitation and put a bowl in front of him, and something about the simplicity of it sat in him like an ache. He had not had this in a long time. He was not entirely sure he had ever had it, or if what he remembered from before the ship, before the famine, before everything, was real or just the shape of something he'd invented to fill the space where it should have been.

He looked at his bowl.

"Thank you, Nóra," he said.

She waved it off and picked up her cup.

Nóra had arrived in New York in 1848 at age twenty, pregnant. She raised four children in the Five Points, buried two of them,. and built a boarding house on Mulberry Street that became an unofficial Fenian safe house, meeting room, and postal address for Brotherhood correspondence that couldn't go through official channels.

She was part of the operation's invisible infrastructure. She laundered money through her boarding house accounts, keeping donations and fundraising efforts clandestine. Among many other services, she also sewed Brotherhood insignia into the lining of their coats and uniforms.

Later that day, Seamus and Rónán had reported what had transpired to their superiors in the Brotherhood. They did not respond kindly to instances of anti-Irish discrimination or harassment. A counter-action was planned.

The following weekend, an organized raid took place in the general area where Seamus and Rónán had been attacked. Dozens of Fenians, armed with handguns and shillelaghs, streamed through the backstreets and alleyways. They converged on the businesses and properties of known transgressors. Windows were broken. Stores were looted. The homes of policemen who had arrested any Irish in recent weeks were likewise targeted. Scuffles and shootouts took place, and revenge was had.

4

Féile Cheilteach - Celtic Festival

The *brat Bríde* were all out all through the neighborhood.

They hung from the lintel and the window frames in pale, frost-stiffened lengths, barely moving in the February stillness. Seamus stopped on the pavement and looked up at them. The boarding house behind them was solid brick, gas lamp on the corner, a cart horse standing patient at the kerb further down the street. New York in every direction.

But the cloth strips were not New York. They were something older, something that had crossed the Atlantic folded inside a woman's memory and unpacked itself here on Mulberry Street without apology.

For a moment, he was ten years old again. In his mind, he saw a stone cottage outside Mayo, the air smelling of peat and wet grass, his mother's hands threading strips of her old shawl through the door latch before bed. *For Brigid,* she'd said. *She'll bless the cloth as she passes in the night.*

The cart horse shifted its weight and the sound brought him back. February 1866. The cloth strips turned in the wind.

He knocked.

Nóra opened the door already talking.

"Seamus. Come in, come in, you'll freeze standing there." She pulled the door wide. "Leave your boots on the mat."

He unlaced them, pulled off his scarf, and lifted his coat from his shoulders. The rack beside the door already held three other coats. He hung his beside them.

"Tea's on," she called from the kitchen. "Hot enough to take the frost off."

He followed her voice. The kitchen was warm and smelled of something dried and green, faintly grassy, not entirely unlike the inside of a barn. He stopped in the doorway.

The table was covered. Long dried reeds lay in loose bundles, some already separated into individual stalks. Others had been sorted and dampened, a shallow basin of water keeping them supple. Three half-finished crosses sat at the near end, their centers bound with twine, their arms still uneven and splayed. A small pile of off-cuts littered the floor beside the nearest chair.

Nóra set a cup in front of him and sat down across the mess with the brisk efficiency of a woman who considered chaos an intermediate stage rather than a problem.

"Excuse the state of it," she said, picking up a bundle of reeds. "Sit, if you can find the room."

He moved a bundle aside and sat. "Saint Brigid's crosses."

"Soon to be." She held one up, turning it. "These are Hudson reeds, not true rushes. I had a man bring me a bundle from the riverbank last autumn. Not the same." She set it down. "But it's what we have."

"I've not made one since I was a boy."

"Then you'll help me finish these." She slid a dampened bundle toward him. "Take four. Fold the first one at the center."

He picked up four reeds, thin and slightly waxy, still holding a curve from how they'd been bundled. He folded the first one and held the crease between his thumb and forefinger.

"Now thread the second one through the fold," Nóra said without looking up from her own work. Her fingers moved with the certainty of long practice, bending, threading, turning the cross a quarter rotation. "Perpendicular like."

He threaded the second reed. It slipped. He tried again, the linen wrapping still on his palm from two days prior making his fingers thick and slow. The reed kinked and he swore under his breath.

"The other way." Nóra reached across and turned his work without ceremony. "There."

He tried again. The cross held its shape for a moment before one arm sagged.

"You've a soldier's hands," she said. Not unkindly. "Ease off a bit."

He loosened his fingers and the weave sat better. Nóra watched, corrected the angle of his third reed with one finger, and returned to her own work.

"Brigid is the saint of women," she said, bending a stem. "Of healers and poets and midwives. Fugitives too. Before she was a saint, Brigid was once something like a goddess. The Church tried to do away with her, but the people kept telling her story anyway because some things won't be told otherwise." She paused to dampen a reed in the basin. "The first of February is hers. The old ones called it *Imbolc*. The first breath of spring, even if the ground's still hard. She walks the earth the night before, blessing what she passes, bringing about the thaw."

Nóra went on about the saint, the old country, and Irish customs. She talked about Saint Brigid's Day in Ireland, back when she was a girl. She described the Biddy Boy processions, men dressed in straw costumes going from house to house carrying a small straw doll, called *brideóg,* collecting food and money. It was considered unlucky to refuse them, Nóra explained.

Seamus looked down at his own cross. It was lopsided, one arm noticeably shorter than the others, but it held together. He turned it once, checking the center knot, and found it solid enough.

"Is it fit?" he asked.

Nóra examined it with the critical eye of a woman who knew the difference. "It'll do."

He took that for the praise it was.

When they were done she handed him the finished cross and pointed at the ceiling, at a low beam that crossed the kitchen from wall to wall. He stood on the chair she indicated, reached up, and pushed the looped twine over a nail already waiting there. The cross settled against the dark wood. Higher up, there were older crosses from previous years.

He stepped down, and they looked at it together.

"Will you stay for supper?"

Nóra need not have asked. Seamus never rejected her invitation.

She prepared a traditional Irish dish called colcannon, made from mashed potatoes, cabbage, and freshly churned butter. It was served with fresh bread. Dessert was Seamus's choice of apple cakes or barm brack. He chose the apple cakes. Seamus savored every bite, sharing Nóra's table with the other guests of the boarding house.

As they ate, a conversation spread about an upcoming festival, organized by the Fenian Brotherhood. It was set to occur in a few weeks time, occupying a timely slot between Saint Brigid's

Day and Saint Patrick's Day.

Drawing upon Celtic origins, the four day festival was to be called *Oimelc,* meaning "ewe's milk," coinciding with the start of the lambing season and the coming of spring. As it was advertised, the gathering would feature music, dancing, sports, art, poetry, and plenty of food and drink as well. It was a gathering for all classes and ages, and the Scottish-Americans were invited too.

As a member of the brotherhood, Seamus's attendance and full participation was expected. In preparation, he visited a barbershop for a fresh haircut, and later that day, he had a tailor sew up the rips in his best jacket.

* * *

The hall on Worth Street was the largest Irish-owned building in lower Manhattan, and tonight it was full to the brim.

Seamus heard it from the street, the pipes already going, the low throb of a *bodhrán* underneath, and above everything the collective noise of several hundred people existing at close quarters with food and drink and no particular reason for restraint. He straightened his jacket on the steps.

Rónán appeared at his elbow from nowhere, as was his habit.

"You look like a man attending his own trial."

"You look like you dressed in the dark."

"I did." Rónán held the door open. "After you."

The warmth hit first, then the smell of tallow and pine boughs and roasting meat. Then the noise closed over them like water. The hall ran sixty feet or more from door to far wall, and every foot of it was occupied. Green boughs hung from the rafters in long swags, and someone had woven rushes through them in loose spirals. Candles burned in rows along the window ledges and on the long tables that ran down the center of the room, their light catching the faces of men and women packed in shoulder to shoulder, children weaving between adult legs, old women in dark shawls occupying the chairs along the walls like a panel of judges.

Finn's broadsides covered every vertical surface. The sunburst harp blazed from the far wall above the low stage, eight feet across, the colors vivid against the whitewashed brick. Smaller ones lined the sides. In among them, newer work that Seamus hadn't seen before.

A fiddle shrieked through a fast reel from the corner of the stage and four or five couples cleared a space on the floor without being asked, launching into a set dance that sent the children scattering away. Someone pressed a cup into Seamus's hand. He didn't see who. He drank. It was good Irish whiskey, better than he usually encountered, and it sat warm in his chest.

After some convincing, Seamus joined the dancing, his body moving naturally to produce reels and jigs. He danced with a young woman, a second-generation Irish-American girl from the Bronx, dark-haired and quick on her feet. She laughed at his footwork and didn't let him lead properly, which he found unexpectedly delightful.

Rónán had already found someone he knew, clasping a broad man's hand and pulling him into an embrace, laughing at something. The room absorbed them all without effort.

Seamus, thinking proactively, ceased dancing before getting too sweaty. After a graceful exit, he drifted toward the far end of the hall, stopping to greet men he recognized, Brotherhood members, some of them, others simply neighbors from Mulberry Street, men he'd seen at Mass or passed on the stairs of the boarding house. A pair of Scots in good wool coats stood together near the food table with the slightly formal posture of invited guests uncertain of the customs, and one of them caught his eye and raised his cup. Seamus raised his back.

The music shifted. The fiddler wound the reel down and a set of uilleann pipes filled the silence that followed, something slower, a tune Seamus half-recognised from childhood without being able to name. It moved through the hall and the conversations around him softened without stopping, people talking quieter without knowing why.

Then Finn stepped onto the stage.

He didn't announce himself. He simply walked to the front of the low platform, stood still for a moment, and the room noticed him. That was a skill Seamus had observed before, the ability to fill a space not with volume but with attention, to make everyone present feel that something was about to happen worth turning toward.

Finn's coat was a deep green, the pocket square white. He had no notes.

"My friends."

Finn let the two words land before he added anything to them. His voice was a performance instrument and he knew how to tune it to a room. It was not loud, not projected, simply placed, the way you'd set a glass down on a table without a sound.

"The Gaels understood winter."

He paused. The pipes had gone quiet. The room was listening.

"Not the way we understand it now, with our coal stoves and our gaslights and our glass windows keeping the dark at arm's length." He gestured at the hall around them, the candles, the warmth, the bodies pressed together. "Our ancestors understood winter as something that meant to kill you. The cold came in through the thatch and the stone and the door-gaps, and the dark came early and stayed late, and the food you'd put by in autumn was shrinking every day. And you'd ask yourself, sitting there in the dark — *will the light come back? Will the earth soften again? Will I see another spring?*"

He walked the width of the stage slowly, his hands clasped behind him.

"And the answer was — *you do not know.* You never know. You only have faith. You hold on, and you trust."

Seamus stood still in the crowd with his cup at his side, watching. Beside him, Rónán had stopped talking to whoever he'd been talking to.

"That's what *Oimelc* is about." Finn turned back to face the room. "The first ewes beginning to milk. The first lambs coming wet and trembling into the world. The ground still hard as iron underfoot, the air still sharp enough to cut glass — and yet." He raised one finger. "Life. Arriving anyway. Stubbornly. Without asking anyone's permission."

A few people laughed. A woman near the back said something quiet in Irish and the old women in the chairs along the wall giggled.

"It is God's promise kept," Finn said, and his voice dropped a register, the lightness stripped out of it. "Year after year, the darkness ends. The light returns. The lamb is born. Whatever you endured in the winter — the hunger, the cold, the long nights when you sat there wondering if this was the year the spring did not come — it ends."

The room was very quiet now. Seamus found himself thinking of nothing in particular, which was unusual for him, and which he recognized as the sensation of being spoken to directly rather than addressed.

Finn made it political.

"Ireland," he said, "is still in the long winter of foreign occupation."

No one breathed.

"For centuries, the cold, bleak presence of British tyranny has kept our people indoors, sheltering from harsh conditions." His jaw tightened. "They took the land. They suppress our language. They starve us, imposing winter-like conditions on foodstuffs and rations."

Somebody in the back of the room yelled out "Fuckers!" and the man next to him added, "Scum!"

"But we endure!" Finn spread his arms. "Every person in this room is a lamb that arrived anyway. Every Irish child born on this soil, every man who crossed that ocean and kept his faith and kept his language and kept the songs — that is the *Oimelc*. That is the thaw beginning!"

The crowd began to stir.

"The spring is coming for Ireland!" Finn's voice carried now without effort, reaching the far walls, the old women in their chairs, the Scots by the food table who had gone completely still. "It is our glorious national revival. It has not come yet. But it *is* coming. And when it does, when those clouds of oppression finally break, it will be because men and women held on through the dark. Held on, and kept faith, and did not surrender."

He stood quiet for a moment. Then he smiled, and the room came back into itself.

The applause began at the back and moved forward like a wave. Rónán whistled loudly. The old women nodded slowly in their chairs. The two Scotsmen called out "Unite the Clans! A free Ireland and an independent Scotland!"

Seamus clapped with the rest of them, and the sound of it

filled the hall.

Finn raised both hands and the applause ebbed.

"Brothers and sisters." He turned toward the wing of the stage, then back to the crowd, and the tone in his voice shifted into something more formal, more deliberate. "It is my great honor, on this night of *Oimelc*, to introduce to you the men who made this festival happen. The 'founding fathers' of our Brotherhood. The architects of what is to come."

The room had gone very still once more, onlookers waiting respectfully.

"A gentleman and a scholar." Finn extended one arm toward the side of the stage. "The founder of the Fenian Brotherhood in America, a man who has devoted every year of his life and every penny of his considerable inheritance to the cause of Irish freedom — Mr. John O'Mahony."

O'Mahony walked out from the wing with the deliberate unhurried pace of a man accustomed to rooms falling quiet around him. He was tall and lean, with a high forehead and dark eyes set deep beneath heavy brows. His beard was iron-grey and full, his coat plain but well-made. He carried himself not with the theatrical gravity of a performer but with something quieter and more difficult to manufacture, the settled weight of a man who had been doing this for twenty years and intended to keep doing it until it was done or he was.

He nodded to the crowd once. No smile. No wave. The acknowledgment of a man receiving something he felt obligated rather than entitled to accept.

The applause was enormous.

Seamus brought his hands together hard. Beside him, Rónán's whistle cut through the noise. O'Mahony, the scholar-soldier. The man who had fought in '48 in Ireland, exiled himself to

Paris, crossed to New York, and then devoted what remained of his wealth to building the organization that Seamus had sworn his oath into. Standing there on the low stage in the candlelight of a rented hall on Worth Street, he looked precisely like what he was: a man who had sacrificed everything for a cause that had not yet repaid him.

O'Mahony took a seat at the side of the stage, and Finn stepped forward again.

"The Pride of Ohio." Finn let the phrase sit a moment. "A veteran of the Bloody Tenth, Chief Signal Officer to General Thomas, and the man who broke James Stephens out of prison with nothing but nerve and a good hat — Captain Thomas J. Kelly."

Kelly came out sharper than O'Mahony, quicker on his feet, with the compact energy of a man half-assembled from springs. He was perhaps thirty, clean-shaven except for the goatee that Seamus had heard about before he'd ever seen the man. His facial hair was purposefully grown to conceal the jaw that a Confederate bullet had rearranged at Carnifex Ferry. His eyes moved across the crowd fast and professionally, the habit of a signal officer reading terrain.

He raised one hand to the room. Not a wave, a salute, clipped and precise.

The crowd roared. The Scotsmen near the food table were clapping over their heads.

Kelly sat beside O'Mahony, leaned across, and said something in the older man's ear. O'Mahony's expression didn't change but he dipped his chin slightly, which appeared to satisfy Kelly.

Finn stepped to the front of the stage once more. He paused a beat longer this time, building the room's attention to a finer point before releasing it.

"And finally." His voice dropped, almost intimate, as though what he was about to say was too large for volume. "A man who lost his arm at Fort Donelson and returned to command before the wound had closed. A man the Confederacy could not stop, and who the British Empire would do well to fear." He looked directly at the crowd. "Colonel Thomas W. Sweeny."

Sweeny walked out with his empty left sleeve pinned flat against his coat and his chin up, and the room came apart.

The sound was different from what had greeted the other two. Raw, less ceremonial, the noise of men who recognized one of their own. Veterans were on their feet throughout the hall, some of them calling out unit names, the 69th, the 88th, the Irish Brigade, others simply shouting without words.

Sweeny stood at the front of the stage and let it happen. He was stocky and broad-necked, with a face like a clenched fist and eyes that held a permanent combative light.

Seamus clapped until his palms stung. The scar along his jaw pulled tight where the skin had never quite softened the way it should have, and he didn't notice. He was watching Sweeny stand there on the stage, one-armed and immovable. Seamus admired these men, who filled the room with pride and recognition.

Finn let the applause for Sweeny settle, then raised one hand, and the hall went quiet again.

"There is one more name." His voice had changed register. No performance in it now, something stripped back and plain. "A name that belongs in this room even though the man himself cannot be with us."

He turned slightly toward the three seated men, then back to the crowd.

"Michael Corcoran." He said it simply, without preamble.

"Co-founder of this Brotherhood. Colonel of the 69th New York. A man who refused to march his regiment for the Prince of Wales when he came to America, and faced court martial for it..." Finn paused. "A man who was taken prisoner at Bull Run and spent twelve months in Confederate hands and came out still fighting."

The hall was absolutely still. Even the children had stopped moving.

"He did not live to see this night." Finn's jaw was set. "He fell in Fairfax in December of sixty-three. Taken from us too soon, but the Lord had urgent need for him up above." He looked up toward the heavens for a moment. "Michael Corcoran never stopped. Not once. From the day he left Sligo, to the day we buried him, that man gave everything he had to his people, to this country as well as Ireland, and he asked for nothing back."

Seamus looked at O'Mahony. The older man sat with his hands folded in his lap and his eyes somewhere in the middle distance. His face had not changed, but the stillness of it was different now, heavier, the stillness of a man holding something still inside himself.

Finn let the silence stand for a long moment. Then he said quietly:

"He was one of us. He was the best of us. And we remember him."

Hats came off across the hall. Men bowed their heads. Seamus removed his cap and held it against his chest. Beside him, Rónán did the same without a word. They had served with Corcoran during the war, and knew his measure well.

Seamus thought of the 69th's colors going forward at Fredericksburg, thought of the men who'd carried them and fallen. Corcoran had built that regiment. Had breathed life into it. The men Seamus had marched beside, the men whose names he still carried, had marched under a legacy that Corcoran made.

He bowed his head and said nothing.

The three men sat together across the prepared chairs, received the last of the applause, and when the noise finally subsided, they each rose in turn to deliver their prepared remarks.

O'Mahony spoke first. His voice was measured and precise, the cadences of a scholar who had spent years translating old Gaelic texts, every phrase weighted and placed.

"We are not a mob. We are not a rabble." He looked across the hall with his deep-set eyes. "We are the Irish people, organized and purposeful, and we will conduct ourselves accordingly in everything that is to come."

Kelly followed him. "This organization was formed with intention. From the beginning, we have been moving towards a singular goal. That is of course, the establishment of a free Irish Republic."

O'Mahony had more to add. "Yes. And to that effect, we have been building. This organization now has many thousands of members and powerful connections. We have raised significant funds from generous backers and true believers in our cause... Material to wage the struggle has also been made available to us—"

Colonel Sweeny raised his one remaining hand, quietly signaling for O'Mahony to halt that line of discussion. O'Mahony yielded, allowing Sweeny to take over.

Colonel Sweeny stepped to the front of the stage.

He didn't raise his voice gradually, didn't build to it. He simply opened his mouth and filled the hall, the way a man accustomed to making himself heard over artillery fire fills any space he enters.

"As of this week, I have resigned my commission with the United States Army."

The hall went very still.

Sweeny's single hand was at his side, closed into a fist. "At the behest of this Brotherhood, and with the blessing of Almighty God, I have laid down that commission so that I may devote what years remain to me to a single purpose."

He looked across the crowd. His eyes moved the way a general's eyes move across a map, reading contours, assessing ground.

"The formation of the Army of the Irish Republic."

The eruption was immediate and total. Young men were on their feet before the sentence had fully landed, some of them grabbing each other's arms, some simply standing and roaring. A group near the back began hammering the table with their fists in unison. The two Scotsmen were on their feet as well, their reserve dissolved entirely.

Seamus felt the sound go through him like a charge. He was standing before he'd decided to stand.

Beside him, Rónán had both arms in the air.

Sweeny let it run. He stood at the front of the stage with his pinned sleeve and his clenched fist and let the room spend itself, and when it finally ebbed he raised his hand.

"This army will assemble. It will train. It will be led by men who have already proven themselves on the battlefield of this nation's war." His jaw set hard. "And in the summer, we will launch a grand strategic campaign that the British Empire will not soon forget!"

He said nothing further. He stepped back from the edge of the stage and resumed his place among the others, and his silence was more compelling than another ten minutes of speech would have been. The crowd understood that the details were not for tonight, that what had been offered was intention and the man behind it, and that both were sufficient.

Finn was already moving.

He crossed the stage with his coat open and his hands out, as though gathering the room toward him by feel.

"You've heard from the Colonel." His voice was warm now, the formal register gone. "You know what's being built. And you know, every man in this hall knows, what needs to be done."

He reached into his coat and produced a folded sheet. He held it up. Even from where Seamus stood he could see the sunburst harp printed across the top.

"This is a call to arms. Recruitment!" Finn looked across the crowd. "If you are a man of fighting age. If you have served in the last war or if you have not, but you are willing to learn and to work. If you swore the oath or if you are ready to swear it now." He lowered the paper. "Come forward."

The movement started at the front and spread back through the hall. Young men peeled away from the crowd and pressed toward the stage where Brotherhood men had materialized with pens and ledgers. The queue formed fast, a dozen deep within moments, then two dozen, the men jostling forward with the specific energy of people who have been waiting for permission to act and have finally received it.

Seamus looked at Rónán. He was already moving. Seamus followed.

The queue shuffled forward. Around him the noise was different now, lower and purposeful, men talking in short sentences about units and experience, a few of them already calculating the logistics of their absence. An older man near

Seamus crossed himself and rejoined the queue. A boy of perhaps seventeen stood ahead of him with his shoulders squared and his jaw set in an expression of determined manhood that made him look older than he was.

When Seamus reached the table, a Brotherhood man with a ledger looked up at him.

"Name."

"Seamus McKenna."

The pen moved. "Prior service?"

"69th New York Infantry. Four years."

The man wrote without looking up. He turned the ledger and pushed it across the table with his finger at the relevant line.

Seamus picked up the pen. The nib was worn and the ink came out slightly thick. He signed his name in the ledger, his handwriting small and deliberate, each letter placed.

He set the pen down and stepped back from the table. Rónán was already done, standing with his hands in his pockets, watching the queue continue to grow behind them.

"Well then," Seamus said.

"Soldiers once again," Rónán replied. "One more war. This one's for Éire."

5

Druileáil - Drill

The muster order arrived on a Tuesday, hand-delivered to each man by a Brotherhood courier who did not stay for tea. All were told to make their way to a farm in Delaware County. Two days' travel, first by rail and then by wagon. Every recipient was expected to report for duty before the week was out.

The valley came into view in the late afternoon of the second day, when the wagon crested a low ridge and the driver pulled his horses to a slow walk down the far slope. Below them, spread across the flat ground between two tree lines, was a property that had once been a humble dairy farm. Now, it was a military base.

Tents in long rows. Cook fires. A barn and two outbuildings with men moving in and out of them in a steady stream. Wagon trains queued along a rutted track, their loads covered in oilcloth, here and there a corner lifted to reveal stacked rifle crates or folded canvas or the dull gleam of ammunition boxes nested in straw. A drilling square had been staked out in the east field, and even from the ridge Seamus could see the formations moving through their evolutions, the distant bark of commands carrying up on the air.

"Sweet Mary." Rónán leaned out from the wagon bench. "They've actually done it. We have an army of our own."

Seamus saw hundreds of men, possibly thousands. Young ones mostly, Irish faces and American ones, born in County Clare or born in Chicago, but carrying between them the energy of men who had decided to take action and were no longer waiting.

They checked in at a folding table outside the main farmhouse, where a Fenian officer in a good coat sat with a ledger open before him. He ran a finger down a column, found Seamus's name, then Rónán's, made two marks, and directed them to Battalion C without looking up.

"Cooke's outfit. Barn, east side. He'll sort you."

Seamus and Rónán turned to exit, but were stopped.

"Wait wait wait!" the officer called after them. "Before you report to your unit, you must be cleared for service. Go and visit the medical tent first. It's on the south side of the farm, you can't miss it."

Inside the medical tent, Seamus and Rónán became acquainted with Dr. Cornelius Shaughnessy, who checked them for infirmities, fever, and lice. Dr. Shaughnessy, originally from Galway, served for three years as a regimental surgeon with the Army of the Potomac. By Appomattox, he had amputated more limbs than he could count and had settled into a deep melancholy that nearly every Civil War surgeon carried like a second shadow.

Dr. Shaughnessy said little, and after a brief exam, he cleared the two men, marking them down as fit for duty. Having passed this checkpoint, they were sent on to their unit.

Liam Cooke was not a tall man, but he occupied space. He

stood at the entrance of the barn with his arms crossed and watched the new arrivals approach with an expression that suggested he had already taken their measure and the result was provisional at best.

His face was made of stone. Seams at the corners of his eyes, a jaw that looked as though it had been set against something for a very long time and had stayed that way. His uniform was clean and squared away.

"McKenna." He looked at Seamus. "69th New York?"

"That's right."

His eyes moved to Rónán. "You as well?"

"Through and through," Rónán said.

"Good lads. I've got boys in this unit who've never fired a rifle at anything that shot back. I've got men who think this is a brotherhood picnic. I've got three weeks to make soldiers out of the lot before we cross." He turned and walked into the barn. "Follow me."

The barn held two dozen men on straw pallets, their kit laid out beside them with varying degrees of order. Cooke walked the length of it without looking back, pointing out the water barrel and the location of the cook fire where the evening meal was already being ladled out. He said everything once.

"Eat. Sleep. We start at first light." He paused at the barn door. "Any man who can't keep up on the drill square gets a second chance. Any man who can't keep up on the second chance is dropped from my unit and reassigned to the reserve. Any questions?"

"None, sir."

Cooke walked out.

Rónán waited until the footsteps faded. "Charming man."

Seamus said nothing. He had known men like Cooke in the

69th, sergeants who kept their companies alive through sheer refusal to permit otherwise. He had not always liked them. He had always, in the end, been grateful for them.

Cooke had begun his military service as an enlisted man, starting out as a lowly Private and ending as First Sergeant. Despite serving heroically in both the Mexican-American War and the Civil War, Cooke was routinely passed up for promotion by his superiors, who never seemed to appreciate his full value. Cooke ascended into Commissioned Officer status upon joining the Army of the Irish Republic. Colonel Sweeny himself had personally selected Cooke to lead the vanguard, and bestowed upon him the rank of Major.

Dinner was Army Soup: thin, salty, with floating islands of something that had probably been a turnip before it surrendered. Seamus ate every morsel and soaked the rest up with bread. He had learned early in the war not to refuse food when it was offered.

He bedded down in the hay as the last light left the sky above the barn's open loft, pulling his blanket around him. The sounds of the camp settled around him. He could hear low voices, the creak of wagon wheels somewhere across the field.

He pressed his hands together.

Lord, keep us. Keep us whole and purposeful. Guide our path, Father. Amen.

Sleep took him fast.

The battle had no order to it. It never did, in dreams.

He was at Fredericksburg again, then Gettysburg, then somewhere that was neither, a field that kept changing its geography the moment he tried to orient himself. Men went down around him. Faces he knew, faces he had not thought of in years, people and places rising and then dropping out of the world. He fought through all of it, mechanically, bayonet and rifle and the terrible close work that he never spoke of to anyone, his body doing what it had been trained to do while the part of him that was still a boy from Mayo stood somewhere apart and watched.

Then the cavalry charged.

The rider came out of smoke on a grey horse, enormous, the animal's hooves throwing up clods of black earth. The sabre was in hand, already swinging. Seamus raised his rifle and the rifle was not there. He raised his arm instead. The blade came down in a bright arc.

He woke.

The barn was dark, the only light a thin scattering of stars through the gaps in the roof boards. His heart was running hard and his shirt was soaked through. He pressed one hand flat against the hay beside him, grounding himself in the texture of it.

The scar along his jaw burned. Not pain exactly, more like a memory the body kept independent of the mind. He pressed two fingers to it and held them there until the heat faded.

Around him, the battalion slept. Someone across the barn was snoring with tremendous commitment. Outside, the night was enormous and still, the valley folded in darkness, the camp quiet.

Seamus lay back. He stared at the stars through a crack in the roof and slowed his breathing by degrees, the way a man walks back from a ledge. After some time, he returned to rest.

* * *

Cooke had them on the field before the mist had lifted from

the valley floor.

The drill square was a rectangle of churned earth staked at its corners with iron pegs and rope, and overnight's rain had turned the surface into dark mud. Every step sucked at the boot heel and released it with a wet smack. Within ten minutes of the first formation, the men's trouser legs were black to the knee.

"Column of fours," Cooke called from the edge of the square. "Left wheel, march."

The unit attempted it. The result was not a wheel. It was a gradual collapse of geometry, the rear ranks concertina-ing into the middle as the left file turned too sharp and the right file failed to compensate. A man near the back walked directly into the man ahead of him and knocked him sideways into the mud.

Cooke said nothing. He let it finish failing, then walked into the middle of it with his broadsword hanging at his side.

"Again."

They went again.

Seamus had drilled enough to know what a unit in formation was supposed to feel like — a single body with a single intention, every man's timing borrowed from the man beside him. What this felt like was forty individuals making forty separate decisions about where their feet should go next, all of them slightly wrong.

His own boots kept finding the soft spots. The mud grabbed and released and grabbed again, breaking cadence, throwing off the count. He compensated, adjusting the length of his stride, but the man to his left had no such instinct and lurched wide on every step, forcing Seamus to contract or collide.

"Dress the line." He said it without looking. "Give me your

shoulder, not your elbow."

The man shuffled inward.

It was marginally better. Not good.

On the third attempt at a right-face column march, the recruit immediately behind Seamus — a slight figure, young, his jacket two sizes too large across the shoulders — stepped on the back of Seamus's boot on the pivot and stumbled hard into the man beside him, starting a small chain of disorder that rippled forward through the rank.

Cooke appeared as though he had been waiting behind the air itself.

The flat of the broadsword connected with the boy's hindquarters with a crack that carried across the entire square. The boy yelped. It was a sharp, involuntary sound, more shock than pain, and straightened so fast his heels nearly left the ground.

Seamus glanced left. Rónán's face was intentionally composed, his eyes fixed dead ahead with the effort of a man trying to contain a cathedral bell inside a matchbox.

Seamus looked forward again and refocused his steps.

"Straighten your line," he said quietly to the boy who'd been struck, who was now standing rigidly upright with two spots of color in his cheeks. "Step off on the left. Count it in your head if you have to. One-two, one-two."

"I was," the boy said, with feeling.

"You weren't. Left foot first. Try again."

They went through the wheel twice more, and both times the boy held the count and the line held its shape. Not elegant. Functional.

Cooke ran them through formation drill until mid-morning, then shifted to individual movement — advance, halt, ground, rise — which the mud made into a particular sort of misery. Men came up from the ground coated to the chest. At one point a man's boot came entirely free of the suction and he continued forward in his stocking foot for three paces before Cooke's voice pinned him where he stood.

The experienced men fared better in principle and worse in practice, because the inexperienced ones clustered around them, seeking orientation the way iron filings seek a magnet, which meant the veterans spent as much energy avoiding collisions as they did drilling.

"Your left, not mine," Seamus said to a broad man from Boston who kept drifting toward him on every advance.

"I know which way left is."

"Then go there."

By the time Cooke called the halt for water, the mud had claimed two canteens, one hat, and whatever goodwill the men had arrived with. They stood in loose clusters at the edge of the square, passing the water pail, their breath coming in clouds in the cold air.

The boy came to stand near Seamus, keeping a careful yard of distance, as though he wasn't entirely sure of his reception.

Seamus handed him the pail. "You held the count, the last two runs."

"Helped to have something to think about besides the cold." He drank, wiped his mouth with his wrist. "And the sting."

Rónán, who had materialized beside Seamus with the silent ease of long habit, took the pail and gave the boy a look of solemn sympathy. "I've had worse from a nun with a ruler. At least Cooke's arm is honest about what it intends."

The boy almost smiled.

"What's your name?" Seamus said.

"Pádraig Connelly." He straightened slightly, the reflex of someone who'd said the name in formal company before. "Most folk call me Patch."

Rónán studied him over the rim of the pail with the unhurried attention of a man doing arithmetic. "And how old are most folk calling you, Patch?"

A pause. Brief but legible.

"Old enough."

"That's not a number," Rónán said pleasantly.

Another pause, longer. Patch looked at the mud on his boots. "Sixteen."

Seamus looked at him properly for the first time. The jacket too large. The face unlined. A boy's hands on a man's canteen.

"Go home, boy."

The youth's chin came up immediately. "I can fight same as any man here."

"I don't doubt it, but you've got some more living to do first."

"My brother fought in the war. He was at Cold Harbor." The words came out flat and certain, stripped of any request for sympathy. "All the men in my family are fighters, rebels, and soldiers, going way back."

Seamus said nothing for a moment.

"I know what Cold Harbor cost and perhaps I knew your brother," he said finally. "That's why I'm telling you to go home."

"And I'm telling you I won't." Patch met his eyes without flinching. The jaw was set in a way that had nothing performative about it. "Sir."

The last word was added neither as deference nor as sarcasm. Simply as punctuation, marking the end of the discussion.

Seamus looked at Rónán. Rónán looked at the sky.

"He's made up his mind sounds like," Rónán said.

Seamus exhaled through his nose. He looked at Patch and weighed what he saw against what he knew, and found that the scales did not tip cleanly in either direction.

"Stay close to us, boy," he said. "And ye may live to see seventeen."

Patch nodded.

"And get a jacket that fits."

* * *

The rifles arrived on a Monday morning, stacked in long crates packed with straw and grease cloth, each one wrapped individually and smelling of the factory. Brotherhood men unloaded them from the wagon bed in pairs while Cooke stood with his arms folded and watched.

The crates bore no markings beyond a stencilled number sequence, but the moment the first grease-cloth wrapping came away, Seamus knew them.

Springfield rifle muskets. The Model 1861, forty inches of browned barrel and polished walnut stock, the same weapon he'd carried through four years of mud and blood with the 69th. He'd cleaned that rifle so many times in the field that the sequence had worn grooves into his memory he couldn't have erased if he'd tried.

He turned the weapon over in his hands. The lock plate was clean. The barrel had the particular smell of fresh factory oil, sharp and almost sweet. He checked the bore from the muzzle end, found it bright and unscratched.

Beside him, Patch accepted his own musket from the man working down the line and nearly dropped it. He recovered, gripping the stock with both hands, and looked it over with the respectful uncertainty of someone handling an unfamiliar tool.

"Springfield?" he asked.

"Springfield," Seamus confirmed. "Same rifle that won the war." He ran his thumb along the hammer, then wrapped his hand around the stock just above the trigger guard, feeling the weight settle into his grip like something returning to its proper place. "Heavy at first. You'll get used to it."

"You will learn this weapon," Cooke said, walking the length of the formation. "You will know every part of it by name. You will know what fails first, what fails second, and what you do when it fails in the field." He stopped at the center and looked along the ranks. "We begin with maintenance. Not with firing. Any man who touches his trigger before I say so will spend the evening digging a new latrine ditch."

Seamus went through the maintenance drill, smooth and efficient.

Lock plate first. He drew the hammer to half-cock, tapped the wedge free with the heel of his palm, and drew the barrel away from the stock in a single practiced motion. The parts came apart in sequence — nipple, lock screws, the mainspring released with care — and he laid each piece on the grease cloth before him in a precise row.

Patch watched from his right, rifle in his lap, hands uncertain.

"Start with the lock." Seamus tapped the plate. "Half-cock first, or you'll have a bad morning. Wedge comes out here."

He talked Patch through it piece by piece, keeping his voice low, his hands demonstrating first so the boy could see the motion before attempting it. Patch's fingers moved too fast on the nipple wrench and nearly stripped the thread. Seamus guided his grip without grabbing, adjusting the angle with two fingers until it caught properly.

"Slow is smooth."

Patch nodded and turned the wrench again, careful this time.

By the time Patch had his lock plate free and his parts laid out in approximate order, Seamus had reassembled his own rifle completely. He checked the action once, drew the hammer back, let it down easy.

Across the square, Cooke moved between the men, correcting grip, correcting posture, tapping a man's elbow down with two fingers or redirecting a cleaning rod that was being applied with more enthusiasm than care. He said nothing to Seamus or Rónán, which was its own form of acknowledgement.

The bayonet drill came two days later.

Cooke had erected a line of scarecrows across the far end of the east field. They were rough things, straw-stuffed coats mounted on fence posts, their arms spread, some with sacking heads tied on with rope. They stood in a crooked line, patient and shapeless, the wind moving their empty sleeves.

"Fix bayonets," Cooke said.

The sound ran down the line, the soft scrape and click of blades seating into place, some men managing it cleanly, others fumbling the lock twice before it caught.

"When I give the order, you will advance at the quick-step. You will close the distance, you will drive through the target, you will not stop until I say halt. You are not stabbing at it. You are driving through it and out the other side." His eyes moved along the formation. "Advance."

The unit moved forward in a ragged surge, the scarecrows growing fast from shapes into things with presence. Seamus hit his target clean. The bayonet punched through the coat fabric and into the straw beneath. He pulled the blade free and stepped back and dressed the line without being told.

To his left, Patch drove his bayonet home with a shout that surprised even him, the blade going in deep. When he tried to pull it free, the fabric held for a moment, then tore away from the post in a long ripping sound, and the scarecrow's stuffing came falling out, loose straw and old rags piling up around Patch's boots.

Patch's mentors looked back at the wreckage and heaped praise on the boy.

"Deadly!" Rónán called out.

Seamus agreed. "Patch takes no prisoners!"

Patch stood with the rifle in both hands and the remnants of his target at his feet, his chest still heaving. He looked at the two of them, then down at the straw. "I can do this."

The marksmanship training filled the final days. Cooke set targets at fifty yards, one hundred, and three hundred, rough boards painted white with dark circles at their centers, and walked the line himself as each man fired, watching the round land, making his assessment, moving on.

Seamus shot competently at fifty and a hundred. At three hundred the drift caught him on two of his five shots, the rounds pulling left by a fraction that felt larger on a target at that distance than it had any right to. He corrected his grip on the fourth shot and put it inside the circle. The fifth followed it.

Cooke paused behind him, looked at the target board for a moment, then moved on without comment.

Rónán shot last in their section.

His first round at fifty yards was centered close enough to the mark that Cooke stopped walking and turned back. His first at a hundred landed inside the inner ring. By the time Rónán settled at three hundred yards, a small cluster of men had drifted to watch without quite admitting that was what they were doing.

He fired five rounds in measured sequence, no hurry, adjusting between each shot with small movements of his elbow and shoulder. When Cooke walked out to examine the board, four of the five rounds had grouped inside the inner circle, close enough that a man could cover them with his palm.

Cooke came back and stood in front of Rónán for a moment, looking at the rifle in his hands.

"This lad has an experienced hand."

Rónán smiled and lowered the Springfield. "Cutting down traitors in Virginia will teach ye a thing or two."

Cooke went into the barn without another word and came back carrying a lever-action Henry, the finish still dark and unscratched, the brass fittings catching the afternoon light. He held it out.

Rónán took it in both hands. He turned it over once, ran his thumb along the action, tested the lever. Then he settled it to his shoulder and looked down the sights at nothing in particular.

"She'll do," he said.

"A gift from O'Mahony." Cooke turned back to the line. "The rest of you…repeat the drill. Marksmanship will make or break this army. You *must* be able to hit your target at one hundred yards, or you're out of my unit!"

Seamus reloaded.

Rónán stood beside him with the Henry rifle resting in the crook of his arm, admiring it the way a man admires something he has earned and knows it.

"Don't get smug," Seamus said.

"I would never." Rónán ran a cloth along the barrel. "I am simply appreciating the fact that my talents have finally been recognized by a competent authority."

Seamus raised his rifle and lined up the fifty-yard target.

"Load and aim," Cooke called.

He aimed.

"Fire!"

A cloud of gunsmoke billowed out from their rifles and drifted through the valley.

***

The bugle sounded at dusk.

Not the assembly call Seamus knew from the 69th. This one had a different rhythm, a Brotherhood arrangement, four notes repeated twice. He heard it from the edge of the east field where he'd been cleaning the rifles, and looked up to find every man on the property already turning toward the parade ground.

They came from the barn, from the cook fires, from the latrines and the wagon lines. They came still chewing their evening bread, still pulling their jackets straight, and they assembled on the flat ground in front of the farmhouse with the instinct of men who had spent enough time in uniform to know what a bugle meant when it didn't wait.

Seamus fell in beside Rónán. Patch materialized on his left, his jacket buttoned wrong by one, his hair still flattened from sleep.

"Fix your coat," Seamus said.

Patch looked down and corrected it.

The companies formed in loose regimental order A, B, and

C, with the officers ahead of the line and the sergeants at the flanks. The evening light had gone flat and grey, and the fires threw long shadows across the assembled men.

They wore their mismatched best. Green jackets with yellow trim beside Union blue that had seen two years of hard campaigning, the color washed out to something closer to grey. Blue trousers throughout, mostly, some newer than others. Belt plates caught the firelight, the letters I.R.A. stamped into the brass, polished where the men had taken time and dull where they hadn't. Officers wore epaulets at the shoulder, rank insignia on collar and cuff. A captain two rows ahead of Seamus had a brace of harp buttons running down his green coat, each one catching and releasing light as he shifted his weight. Others still wore what they'd been issued years before, the war-worn blue of the Union Army, its fading a record of the distance they'd already marched.

Cooke walked the length of the formation and said nothing. He had nothing to add. The men were dressed, they were present, they were standing in something approximating order. His silence was approval of a restrained kind.

Then Col. Sweeny came out of the farmhouse.

He came through the door at a pace that made every eye on the field move to him without discussion. He was not a large man, but he moved with total confidence. His left sleeve was pinned at the shoulder, flat and final, the arm gone since Churubusco nearly twenty years past. His uniform was neat, his posture straight, and his face held the expression of a man who had been carrying a very specific plan for a very long time and had arrived at the moment of setting it down.

He took his position in front of the assembled force and looked at them, taking measure of his forces.

The parade ground was quiet.

"Tomorrow," Sweeny said, "we begin our campaign."

His voice carried without effort in the still evening air. It was not a voice built for ceremony. It was a voice built for being heard above things that were trying to drown it out.

"You are the Army of the Irish Republic." He said it without inflation, as a statement of fact. "Not militia. Not irregulars. An army. With its orders, its command, and its cause."

Seamus stood with his rifle at his side and his eyes on the one-armed colonel. Around him, the field was utterly still. Not even the horses moved.

"Britain holds Ireland by a chain that is centuries old. A chain built on starvation, on brutality, on the deliberate destruction of a people. Every man standing in this field has felt the weight of that chain. Every man here knows what it cost to cross an ocean and build a life in a country far from home." He paused. "That ends."

Seamus's jaw tightened.

Sweeny turned slightly, addressing the breadth of the formation. "We've assembled twenty thousand men. Not this field alone. Our brothers mobilize here in New York and also in Vermont. Our contribution will consist of three columns, coordinated, crossing at separate points. United with one final objective."

He let the scale of that settle.

"This is the plan." His voice shifted. The speech was over, the briefing had begun. "The first column, led by John O'Neill, will cross the Niagara and move into Ontario. They will hit the rail lines at Welland and threaten Toronto. They will strike hard and fast, in order to draw out every British soldier and Canadian militiaman that can be moved." He looked along the line. "They are the feint. They go in knowing they are the feint. That is their duty, and it is not a small one."

No man moved.

"While British eyes are on Ontario, a second column, the largest force, will cross from Vermont. It moves north. They will cut the lines of communication and supply between Montreal and Quebec. They will take Canada by the neck, essentially." He held the word. "With this thrust, we will take control of a sizable portion of their territory. We hold it. And we sit across the table from the Crown with something in our hand that they cannot ignore."

The strategic dimensions of the operation were becoming more clear to Seamus and the other enlisted men, who listened on at full attention.

"Your objective," Sweeny said, "is the capital city of Ottawa."

The word went through the formation like a current.

"We take Ottawa. We hold it. And we tell the English, in plain language, that they may have it back in exchange for one thing. One thing only." He looked at the assembled men and his voice did not rise. It dropped. "A free and independent Irish Republic."

Seamus understood the logic of the operation. It was a hostage and ransom play on the international scale, clean, self-evident, brutal in its simplicity. You could not negotiate from nothing. You could not negotiate from grievance. But an army cutting your supply lines and occupying your territory was a different conversation entirely.

Sweeny looked at his troops for a long moment.

"Your sergeants have your orders. Your officers have your routes." His eyes moved along their section of the line. "Make final preparations. We move at dawn."

Major Cooke stood at the front of Battalion C with his hands behind his back, his face giving nothing away.

Colonel Sweeny made his final remarks, snapped a salute, and then turned and walked back toward the farmhouse, and the door closed behind him, and the parade ground remained still for a long moment afterward.

Then, somewhere in the rear ranks, a single man began to sing.

Low at first. Four words of *A Nation Once Again* before the next voice joined it, then another, and the sound swelled out across the valley in the darkening evening, rough-edged and serious, nothing like the pub versions, nothing performed.

Rónán sang with them, carefree and shameless.

Patch, to their left, sang with his eyes straight ahead and his voice cracking on the high notes without apology.

Seamus sang along quietly, accepting whatever lay ahead.

6

An Trasnú - The Crossing

The cannon stood at the head of the parade ground, its barrel pointed north, toward British Canada.

Colonel Sweeny walked to it and the crew stepped aside.

No aide held the match for him. No officer stood at his elbow. With one arm, he took the linstock from the barrel of the gun and touched it to the vent without ceremony or hesitation. The powder took the spark and transformed into fire and smoke.

The report hit Seamus in the chest, a concussive thump that compressed the air and sent a flock of starlings shrieking from the tree line in a black wave. The smoke rolled north in a long white tongue, dissipating in the cold morning air, and the echo came back off the hills a half-second later, diminished, final.

The operation had begun. The army began to move out.

They marched through the morning in column, four abreast, the road hard-packed and pale under an overcast sky. The green flag went up at the column's head, a harp on silk, gold on green, carried by a young man from A Company who had won the honor in a boxing match. It caught the air above the column and held itself there, brilliant and improbable against the grey.

Seamus watched it for a while, then looked back at the road ahead. The night before, Father Declan had made a visit to the staging area. He had come to say a prayer over the boys going to war, and he accomplished this task within an hour of arriving. The clergyman would subsequently be drawn into deeper commitment, egged on by Seamus, Rónán, and the others. After a great deal of social pressure, Father Declan agreed to join them on campaign, although strictly as a pacifist noncombatant, serving exclusively as their chaplain.

Patch pulled alongside Seamus after the first mile of marching, having drifted up from somewhere in the rear. His pack sat high on his narrow shoulders and his stride was good, steady, longer than his frame suggested it should be.

"What do you reckon it'll look like?" Patch said.

"What will?"

"Ireland. When we get back."

Seamus looked at the road. "I couldn't tell you, haven't seen it in years."

"I've never been at all." Patch said it without self-pity, as a plain fact to be accounted for. "My parents used to describe it. My mother said the green there is a different green than here. That you couldn't match it with any paint."

Rónán, on Seamus's right, glanced across. "She was right. It's a wet green. Everything soaked through with it."

Seamus hadn't thought about it in those terms before, but he knew it was true. The Mayo he carried deep in his memory had almost become an ethereal place, something out of a fantasy book.

"The papers will go mad," Patch said. His voice carried the unguarded brightness of someone who had not yet learned to protect his own enthusiasm. "When we take Ottawa. When we sit down across from the Crown with a knife at their supply lines. Every paper in the world will carry it. All of Ireland will know."

"We'll give the world a little shock," Rónán agreed.

"And then, when it's done...when we sail back..." Patch shifted his pack and looked at the green flag above the column's head. "They'll come out to the docks. The whole country. To welcome us home."

Seamus thought about that. Not the crowds, not the docks, but the specific and impossible sensation of standing on Irish soil as a free man, under a free flag. The idea sat in him strangely, at once entirely real and too large to look at directly, the way you couldn't look at the sun without turning.

"Aye," he said. "They will."

"Songs written about us." Rónán raised an eyebrow. "Poems. Finn will produce a masterpiece, no doubt."

"He'll read it at some grand hall in Dublin with that voice of his and half the audience will weep into their hats," Rónán continued.

Seamus mused about the possibilities. Would they be welcomed home as liberators? Heroes? Perhaps they'd raise a statue of Colonel Sweeny when all was said and done.

The road bent north and the column bent with it, the flag swinging on the turn, the tramp of boots steady and unhurried.

"We've reached the crossing," Major Cooke announced once his unit approached the south bank of the Saint Lawrence River. The troops paused there for a moment, naturally gathering in the shaded areas, sipping canteens and catching a breath.

The flag bearer approached the water's edge and waved the colors proudly. It was not vanity; it was a signal to collaborators on the north bank.

Moments later, a timber barge crossed over to them, followed by a pack of smaller river scows. A band of Fenian sympathizers hailing from nearby Glengarry County spoke to Major Cooke and the other soldiers in perfect Scots Gaelic. There were a few words that got mixed up, but otherwise, they helped the Battalion C transit the powerful waters of the Saint Lawrence, ferrying them across in three time consuming trips.

On the north bank, the troops laid low and kept quiet. Six miles away was the Canadian settlement of Cornwall. There was a garrison there, protecting the rail station and a valuable canal that had been built the decade prior. It was a tempting target for the Fenians, but if they engaged the enemy at this stage in the operation, reinforcements would arrive long before the Irish could reach Ottawa. They held their fire and did their best to not draw attention from the locals.

The tree line was forty yards to the north, a dark wall of spruce and birch pressing close to the riverbank. Battalion C had spread into the shade of it, rifles grounded, packs off, the men resting in the particular way soldiers rest, the body horizontal while the mind stays upright.

Seamus sat against a birch trunk with his back to the river, watching the forward perimeter.

Rónán lay beside him, his hat over his face, his breathing slow and even. Patch was fighting against a nap that threatened to overtake him. His chin dropped to his chest, his rifle canted against his shoulder at an angle that would have drawn Cooke's correction.

The forest was quiet. A woodpecker somewhere deep in it, methodical and distant. The river behind them moved with a low, constant sound, impersonal and indifferent to the army sheltering at its edge.

Then the branches moved.

Not wind. The movement had direction to it, a disturbance that tracked from right to left through the undergrowth and then stopped. Seamus had his eyes on it before he had consciously decided to look. His hand found his rifle without thought.

Two men stepped out of the tree line thirty feet to his left.

Young, both of them. Younger than Patch. They wore deerskin leggings and loose shirts, their dark hair long and straight, and they carried themselves with the easy physicality of men who had grown up in this terrain. The shorter of the two carried three large fish on a string. The taller had a hatchet at his belt.

They stopped when they saw the soldiers.

Rónán's hat came off his face in the same instant. He was upright with the Henry rifle half-raised before anyone spoke, his thumb on the hammer.

"Easy," Seamus said quietly.

The two young men had gone very still. Their eyes moved across the soldiers — the rifles, the green jackets, the encampment spreading through the trees — with the focused attention of men cataloguing a threat. The shorter one had shifted his weight onto his back foot. The taller's hand had tightened on the hatchet.

"Easy." Seamus said it again, and this time he directed it toward the two men as much as toward Rónán. He set his rifle down in the grass, slowly, making sure the motion was legible, and raised both palms.

Rónán did not lower the Henry.

"Rónán."

"I see them."

"Lower the rifle."

The Henry came down, slowly, Rónán's eyes never leaving the two figures before them.

Seamus took a careful step forward, keeping his hands visible.

The shorter man said something to the taller. Quick, low, the words shaped by a language Seamus had never heard, consonants running differently than English or Irish, the rhythm of it unfamiliar. The taller man responded without looking away from the soldiers.

"We're not your enemy," Seamus said. He kept his voice level. Unhurried.

The two men watched him.

He touched the green of his jacket with two fingers, then pointed north. "We're here for the redcoats." He gestured, sketching the outline of a soldier's coat with his hands, then shook his head. He pressed his palm to his own chest. "Not your fight. Not with you."

The taller man's expression shifted by a fraction. Something that wasn't quite recognition but was adjacent to it.

Patch had woken beside him and sat motionless, his eyes tracking between the two strangers and Seamus with the alert stillness of a boy trying very hard not to do anything wrong.

Seamus pointed north again. "British." He brought his hands together and then pushed them apart, a breaking motion. "We're going to fight them." He looked at the two men and tried to make his face say what his words could not fully carry. "Not your people, just the English."

It was not enough. He knew it was not enough even as he said it. The words were too small for what he was trying to move across the distance between them, and he lacked the language that would have made it precise. He stood in the gap of that silence and let it be what it was.

The shorter man spoke again to the taller. The taller listened, then looked at Seamus for a long moment, his eyes moving from the green jacket to the raised palms and back.

Then he stepped back.

One step, then another, pulling the shorter man with him by a gesture of his shoulder. They moved back into the tree line. The undergrowth received them, shifted once, and was still.

Seamus stood with his palms still raised for a moment after they were gone.

Rónán let out a breath through his teeth. "Christ."

"Aye." Seamus lowered his hands and looked at the tree line. The woodpecker had started up again, far away.

"Do you think they'll send word?" Patch said, his voice carefully even. "To the garrison at Cornwall?"

Seamus picked his rifle up from the grass. "I don't know."

He looked north through the trees, toward the road they would march when the order came, toward the city that waited beyond it.

"I don't know," he said again, and left it there.

* * *

The column made camp as the last light drained from the sky, settling into the spruce and birch well back from the riverbank where the tree canopy was thickest. No fires within sight of the river. Cooke had made that clear before the first pack hit the ground.

They ate. It was hardtack, salt pork, whatever a man had in his haversack. They gathered in loose clusters among the roots and fallen wood. Cooke moved through the camp once, satisfied himself that the perimeter was set, then came back and lowered himself onto a log at the edge of the group with the deliberate care of a man whose joints had been logging complaints since Vicksburg.

He ate a cold can of beans from his own kit. Nobody spoke to him for a while. Nobody needed to.

Then Patch, who had not yet learned when silence was structural, looked up from his hardtack.

"Sir. A question, if I may. How far away is Ottawa?"

Cooke chewed. Swallowed. Looked at the boy without visible irritation.

"Fifty miles or so. We move north when the rear elements are across and the supply line is secured." He broke a piece of hardtack cleanly along its seam. "Our auxiliary forces and supplies will be brought across when the light returns."

"More men crossing?" Rónán said.

"More men. More ammunition. More everything." Cooke said. "The plan calls for reinforcing the column once a supply corridor is established. If we are to take Ottawa and hold it long enough to negotiate a deal with the Crown, we'll need to keep our forces supplied and well armed."

Seamus listened and said nothing.

"And if the British move before then?" Patch said.

"Then we fight with what we have." Cooke looked at him with the flat patience of a man who had already run this calculation and filed the result. "Which is why I've got half the battalion on rotation watch tonight and the other half sleeping with their boots on."

He finished the hardtack. Dusted his hands on his trousers.

"The river crossing is the critical point," he continued, his voice dropping into the register he used when he was talking through a problem rather than addressing subordinates. "Once we have men and materiel established north of the Lawrence in sufficient number, Cornwall becomes irrelevant. They can't move on us without stripping their garrison. They strip their garrison, the canal is exposed. Plus, the Montreal Column is marching from Vermont. They'll lock down the rail corridor and prevent a rapid response." He looked at the darkness beyond the trees. "The English are methodical. They won't move until they understand what they're dealing with. That gives us a window."

"How wide a window?" Seamus asked.

Cooke looked at him. "Narrow enough to slip in a nasty blow, on the chin, hopefully."

A courier arrived twenty minutes later, pushing through the tree line from the eastern perimeter with the controlled urgency of someone carrying news he'd been told to deliver fast. He was a young lad, Brotherhood courier by the cut of his jacket, his breathing elevated.

He went straight to Major Cooke and said it low.

Cooke's face did not change. He asked one question and received one answer. Then he stood.

"There was a battle… at Ridgeway!" He said it to the group assembled around him, loud enough to carry without carrying further. "The Ontario Column engaged the Canadian militia this afternoon. They drove them back. We won."

The silence lasted perhaps two seconds.

Then it broke.

The sound that moved through the camp was not orderly. It began as one man's shout somewhere to the left, a single raw syllable of disbelief and joy, and it multiplied before the echo had finished, men scrambling upright from their bedrolls, the news moving through the trees person to person faster than the courier could have carried it. Patch was on his feet, his fist raised high, and Rónán beside him, his head thrown back. Someone in the camp started hammering his canteen against a tree root. Two men broke into a sloppy river dance.

"We beat them!" Patch shouted. "On their own soil!"

"Quiet." Cooke's voice came in under the noise like a blade.

Nobody heard it.

"Quiet!" Louder this time, and something in the quality of it, not volume but certainty, the tone of a man who had never once needed to say a thing three times. The order reached the nearest men and moved outward from them.

The camp fell back.

Men stood with grins still on their faces, breathing hard, the joy not gone but contained, held behind their teeth.

"The Ontario Column won a battle." Cooke's voice carried clean in the silence. "A militia engagement." He looked at the faces in front of him, Patch's flushed brightness, Rónán's still-wide eyes, the dozen other men who had stopped mid-celebration. "One skirmish is nothing. Expect a dozen or more such engagements in the days to come. We'll win some and lose others. Keep your bearing and focus on the mission."

He let that sit.

"You'll celebrate when we've done what we came here to do. Until then, you'll keep your voices down and your rifles close and you'll let the Brits wonder what's coming for them."

He sat back down on the log.

The camp settled into its quiet again, slower this time, the energy still present but internal now, running through the men like current through wire rather than breaking the surface.

A stranger appeared in the camp. He had slipped past the night watchmen, penetrated their defensive perimeter and strode confidently to the center. He stopped in front of Liam Cooke. Dim lantern light illuminated the stranger.

He wore an ornate gustoweh atop his head that featured three eagle feathers: two standing upright and one hanging down. Stretched across his broad, muscled chest was a fine buckskin shirt decorated with intricate beadwork. He wore leggings of dark wool trimmed with ribbon and his moccasins were made from moose hide.

The man looked at the Irish-American soldiers gathered there with judgement in his eyes. He said nothing.

Startled, Major Cooke attempted to speak with the stranger. At that moment, a young girl appeared from behind his back. She was small, age twelve perhaps. She spoke to the soldiers in English.

"You are on our land," she said plainly. "You trespass. This is a violation."

Seamus spoke first. "There is a misunderstanding."

The stranger said something to the girl in their native language. She translated it for them.

"You have come to Akwesasne without invitation. The warriors of the Mohawk nation have your camp surrounded. If you have come to make war, you are certain to lose."

Major Cooke spoke for the group. "We are sorry. This is only temporary. We want no trouble with your people. We will soon move on to Ottawa."

"Ottawa?" the stranger repeated the word. The young girl helped him to understand what Cooke had said.

The girl delivered a reply. "We are the Keepers of the Eastern Door. If you wish to pass through our land, you must ask."

Major Cooke, somewhat annoyed, asked the stranger if their column could pass through Mohawk territory on their way to their objective. The stranger was not moved by Cooke's initial request. Through his interpreter, the man demanded that the Irish make an offering of goodwill to the Mohawk nation. Reluctantly, Cooke and the other commanders parted ways with a select number of rifles, handguns, and swords. In total, more than a dozen weapons were handed over, restricting the stockpile of available replacements.

The loss of supply was significant, however, this offering seemed to bridge the gap between the trespassers and the natives. The attitude of the stranger shifted entirely. His warriors emerged from the darkness, themselves relieved that diplomacy had prevailed.

The translator eventually introduced herself as Katsitsienhawi or *She carries the flowers.* She revealed that the stranger was her older brother named Kaientaronkwen meaning *Gathering the Goods.*

Kaientaronkwen was not a selfish man. He reciprocated the gift giving, offering the Irish foodstuffs, a sip of maple-water, and a draw from a ceremonial pipe. The two groups of people mingled for some time, trying their best to communicate and share with one another.

Eventually, Kaientaronkwen and Katsitsienhawi departed, leaving the Irish camp behind. Two Mohawk scouts would remain with the Ottawa Column to ensure that they departed their territory without issue. Major Cooke and the others were happy to have local guides assist them.

Morale amongst the Irish remained high. Their grand strategic objective of freedom, liberty, and dignity for Ireland was within reach, and the men could feel it.

7

Móinteán - Quagmire

The column marched north. For two days, the Army of the Irish Republic trekked across the fertile lowlands north of Cornwall. The men kept a good pace and with the help of local guides and sympathetic collaborators, they covered approximately fifteen miles per day. They passed by a dozen farms and villages, inevitably drawing the eyes of curious onlookers.

As they approached their objective on the third day, the fair and agreeable terrain morphed into something far more adversarial. The outermost perimeter of the Canadian Shield consisted of intercut layers of bogs, hills, thick forests, ponds, lakes, creeks, and the like. Each obstacle collected its tax. Equipment was lost. Boots, blankets, and bullets claimed by breakage. The men paid the toll with their sweat and good spirits.

At a particularly challenging junction, the advance was stalled for several hours. The bog had forced a halt.

The mud and water hid dangers that younger soldiers did not expect or anticipate. Due to a misstep, Patch sank into a mud hole chest deep. He was about to go completely under when

Seamus grabbed the boy's collar and heaved him up a few feet. Rónán had to help them regain their footing.

The bog had no interest in their timeline.

It stretched north from the tree line in a broad, sodden expanse, broken by islands of sedge grass and standing water that reflected the flat grey sky. The ground that looked firm gave way underfoot without warning, and the ground that looked soft sometimes held, which meant every step was a negotiation conducted in bad faith.

Seamus had one hand on the strap of his pack and his eyes on the ground ahead, reading the surface the way he'd learned to read ice as a boy in New York winters. Dark patches. Bright patches. The way certain grass grew only where there was water underneath.

He was mostly wrong.

His left boot sank to the ankle on a step that had looked solid. He pulled it free with a sound like a cork leaving a bottle and planted it somewhere worse. The cold water came in through the seam above the sole immediately.

Behind him, a chain of soft curses marked where Rónán had found the same hole.

A supply cart had bogged entirely, both rear wheels swallowed to the axle. Six men worked at it, shoulders to the frame, their boots churning the muck into something that no longer resembled ground. The cart did not move. The cart had opinions about where it intended to remain.

Major Cooke stood at the cart's edge and looked at it with disdain. He called upon his most qualified resource, a man by the name of Aleksander Wierzbicki. Most folks just called him 'Aleks' or 'the engineer.'

Aleksander was one of the very few men in the column

who was not Irish at all, not even Catholic. He was a Polish immigrant who fought with the Army of the Potomac as a combat engineer and met the Irish Brigade at Spotsylvania. He joined the Fenians not out of Irish solidarity but out of a pan-European revolutionary conviction. Aleksander had cousins actively fighting in the January Uprising against Russia far to the east. To Aleksander, this operation was just the local front in a global war against empire.

To Major Cooke, Aleksander was an indispensable practical man, bringing with him an understanding of river crossings, fortifications, and demolition, among other things. Without Aleksander, the operation had no engineering competence whatsoever.

After observing equipment loss and operational delay, Aleksander leapt into action, taking temporary command override. Under his direction, teams of low ranking soldiers were made to focus entirely on moving the column forward. The correct methods were put to use and the course of advance was modified slightly.

By the evening time, the column began to make progress once more. Exhausted, disoriented, and depleted, the column left the bogs behind and pressed on, driving themselves ever northward, their eyes set on the Ottawa Valley and the capital city nestled within.

Once back on solid ground, Major Cooke ordered the men to pitch a light camp and to eat hearty. They planned to reach Ottawa on the next day's march.

Dr. Cornelius Shaughnessy moved from tent to tent. He spoke to each soldier individually and assessed the condition of the feet. He was absolutely adamant that each man clean their feet, treat any wounds or blisters, and change into clean dry socks. If a man didn't have socks, the doctor gave him some, while supplies lasted.

The camp had settled into itself after the bog. Major Cooke permitted cook fires, so long as they were kept small and low. The men sat close to them in the particular silence of soldiers who had spent every last reserve of physical effort.

Seamus had his boots off. He was examining the sole of the left one, turning it in the firelight, checking the seam where the water had come in. The leather had swollen and softened and the stitching at the heel had begun to pull. He pressed his thumb along the separation and considered how many more miles the boot had left in it.

Rónán dropped down beside him with a tin plate piled with the evening's offering. Hard bread, some dried meat, and a wedge of yellow cheese that had survived the bog with more dignity than most of the men. He balanced the plate on his knee, produced a locket from inside his jacket, and opened it, setting it against his cup where the firelight could reach it.

"Look at her." He said it to nobody in particular, or to both of them, which amounted to the same thing.

Seamus leaned over. Inside the locket, a small oval photograph, the woman's face pale and dark-eyed, her hair pinned up, her expression carrying the particular gravity that long exposures required but which also happened to make her look like she was thinking about something she hadn't told anyone.

"Mariah Jones," Rónán announced. "Twenty-three years of age. Originally from Bridgeport, currently residing in my heart."

Seamus looked at the photograph for a moment. "She's lovely, Rónán."

Patch had appeared on the other side of the fire, his own plate in hand. He craned forward without ceremony to look at the locket.

"All mine," Rónán said, closing it with a soft click and returning it to his breast pocket with the satisfied gravity of a man replacing something irreplaceable.

Patch pulled a piece of dried meat apart with his fingers and chewed it. "Lucky man."

"Extraordinarily," Rónán agreed. He tore a piece of bread. "And yourself, Patch? Is there a girl keeping vigil for you back home?"

Patch's jaw stopped moving for a moment.

"Yes," he said. Then: "Well. No. Not exactly."

Rónán looked up from his bread with undisguised interest.

"There was," Patch said, with the tone of a man who had not intended to admit this and was now committed to it. "A girl in Queens. Her family has a restaurant on Northern Boulevard."

"Italian?" Seamus asked.

"How did you know?"

"Queens."

Patch accepted this logic. "Her name was Lucia. She's..." He turned the piece of dried meat over in his fingers. "She has this way of laughing, like she doesn't intend to and then can't stop herself. Her parents hated me."

"Ah." Rónán settled back on his heels with the expression of a man recognizing a familiar map.

"Her father told her she wasn't allowed to see me anymore. That was back in February." Patch set the meat down on his plate. "She listened to him."

Rónán and Seamus looked at each other across the fire.

"So," Rónán began, with great care and no care at all, "this whole army business..."

Seamus pressed his lips together.

"The marching. The rifles. The bog we nearly drowned in today." Rónán gestured broadly at the camp around them, at the Canadian darkness pressing in on all sides. "All of this…"

Patch's face had gone the color of the fire.

"Is it possible," Seamus said, keeping his voice entirely level, "that somewhere in your thinking, the notion occurred to you that a man who has served in a military campaign might be the sort of man a girl's father can't so easily dismiss?"

The silence that followed was answer enough.

Patch stared at his plate. The color in his cheeks had deepened to something approaching crimson. "That's not the only reason I'm here."

"No," Seamus said. "Of course not."

"I believe in the cause," Patch said, with genuine heat. "I do. I want to fight for Ireland. That's real."

"Absolutely," Rónán agreed.

"But," Patch said, and stopped.

"But Lucia's father needs to understand that Pádraig Connelly is a man of consequence," Rónán said, with great solemnity.

Patch stabbed a piece of meat with unnecessary force. "You're rude. Both of you, mean and rude."

Seamus looked across the fire at the boy's burning face, at the set of his jaw that was trying very hard to reassemble its dignity, and said nothing further. He thought of the girl at the festival on Worth Street. Dark-haired, quick on her feet, laughing at his footwork and refusing to let him lead. He hadn't learned her name.

He turned the boot over in his hands again and checked the heel seam, and let the fire do its quiet work between them.

Major Cooke saw to it that his army rested. They did not

break camp at dawn, as they had in previous days. Instead, the men were permitted to rise slowly, to have breakfast and coffee in preparation for the final day's march.

However, the Irishmen had made a tactical mistake. Canadian loyalists had raised the alarm days ago, having spotted the column marching past their village. The militias had waited for British support, but now they had it. The combined security force had steadily maneuvered to intercept the Irish, and the debacle in the bog gave them enough time to close the gap.

The British and the Canadians had taken up strong defensive positions on a wooded hilltop south of Ottawa. Above them, tall white pines towered over them like a protective cathedral. They made no attempt to hide. Red uniforms were assembled in long lines. Officers rode on horseback, confident and proud, issuing orders and keeping the line tidy. The Union Jack rippled in the wind.

The opposition forces had placed themselves in the direct path of the column. To avoid them, the Irish would need to march many miles in a secondary lane of approach, and this plan would likely be countered as well, they knew. Major Cooke saw no alternative but to assault the hilltop. They had come to fight, and fight they would.

8

Cath Chnoc na nGiumhas - Battle of Pine Hill

The hill was 150 feet of rising ground, scattered with grey rock outcroppings and dry scrub, the slope opening into the white pine treeline at the crest where the red coats waited. Seamus looked at it the way he had looked at Marye's Heights in December of '62 — the stone wall, the sunken road, the long open ground between the ford and the ridge — and felt the same cold recognition settle in his gut.

Prepared ground. Chosen carefully. Men who had been waiting for the fight to come to them.

"Stay close to me," Seamus told Patch without looking at him. "Remember your training and do exactly as you are told."

Patch gripped his rifle and nodded.

The Fenian line dressed itself into a rough assault formation, sergeants moving along the rear, pushing shoulders inward, closing gaps. Cooke walked the front of it bare-faced and unhurried, his broadsword sheathed, his hands at his sides. The obstacle before them was formidable, but the Irish forces, 1,200 in the column, appeared to outnumber the defenders three to one.

"Advance!"

The line stepped off.

The first volley came before they had covered forty yards.

It came from the treeline in a rolling crack, not simultaneous but staggered, sections firing in sequence the way trained men fire when they have been told to sustain and not expend. The sound arrived a fraction after the first men went down. Three casualties in the forward rank, then two more, one of them spinning about before collapsing. The air above Seamus moved. He felt it as a pressure along his left ear, nothing more.

"Close up!" Cooke's voice, from somewhere in the smoke. "Close the line and advance!"

Seamus moved. His boots found the slope and he leaned into it, his rifle angled forward, the treeline pulling closer in increments. Around him the line pressed forward with the particular quality of men who were frightened and moving anyway, which was the only courage that had ever mattered in Seamus's experience. Patch was a half-step behind his right shoulder, breathing loud, his face pale and frightened. Rónán appeared at his left.

"What in God's name is that?"

Seamus followed Rónán's eyes.

At the center of the British position, low to the ground on a wheeled carriage, six barrels arranged in a rotating cylinder caught the evening light like something pulled from a factory floor and placed on a battlefield by mistake. Two men attended it. One at the crank handle, and another at the hopper, feeding the mechanism.

Seamus had heard of it. Read a description once in a newspaper account from the latter part of the war. Had never seen one.

"Christ in Heaven," Cooke said from somewhere behind them. He had kept pace with the assault, his eyes drawn to the same point.

"They have a Gatling Gun," he said, and there was something in his voice Seamus hadn't heard before. Fear. Doubt. A morbid sense of awe.

The crank turned.

The sound was unlike any weapon Seamus had heard. Not a volley, not a report. A mechanical beat, continuous and industrial, the sound of something that did not need to pause and breathe between shots the way a man did. The rounds came across the slope in a sweeping traverse, kicking up dirt in a moving line, and that line found the left flank of the Irish formation and walked through it.

Men came apart.

When a soldier was killed by rifle volley, it was sudden, arbitrary, here and then gone. This was different. This was the weapon's operator making a deliberate, unhurried decision about direction, the gun going where the crew pointed it, indifferent and thorough. The left flank collapsed in seconds, bodies folding, men scattering, breaking left and running back down the slope.

Seamus threw himself into the grass behind a rock outcropping and pulled Patch down with him by the collar. Rónán dropped on his own into the depression beside them, his rifle tight against his chest.

Around them the hillside had become chaos. Men were exchanging fire with the treeline, pouring rounds up into the pines, the smoke thickening fast. A man ten yards to Seamus's right was reloading on his knees, his hands shaking badly, his face the color of old paper. Another crawled downslope on his elbows, something wrong with his leg below the knee.

The Gatling gun swept back the other direction.

"We can't hold here," Rónán said flat against the ground, his mouth pressed close to Seamus's ear.

Cooke appeared at the rock's edge, low and fast, his hand finding Seamus's shoulder.

"Detachment. Right flank. There's brush and timber running up the eastern shoulder of the hill. Take it." His eyes moved to the Gatling position. "Get in behind that thing and neutralize the gunner."

He was gone before Seamus could answer.

"On me." Seamus looked at Rónán, then Patch, then the four other men hugging the earth around the outcropping. "Move low and move fast. Don't stop for anything."

The gap between their position and the brush line was thirty yards of open slope. The Gatling gun had traversed left again, chewing at the center of the Irish line, which meant thirty yards was possible. Seamus read the gun's rhythm the way he had once read Confederate picket rotations, the sweep, the pause, the sweep back.

"Now."

He broke from the rock and ran.

The slope pulled at his legs, the wet grass slick underfoot. Rounds from the treeline snapped overhead, the staggered volley fire from the militia rifles, and he counted his steps without thinking about it, his body making the calculation that his mind was too busy to complete. He hit the brush line hard, shoulder-first into a thorn thicket, branches clawing at his jacket and face, and drove through it until the ground dropped into a shallow draw on the far side.

He turned. Patch came in behind him at a full run, his eyes wide, and dropped into the draw breathing in great heaves. Rónán slid in next, smooth and efficient. The others came in pairs, the last man's boot catching the thorn brush and tearing it sideways as he fell.

Seamus grabbed Patch by the chin and turned his face left, then right. A thin scratch ran from his jaw to his ear, already beading red, but his eyes were clear and tracking.

"All right?"

Patch pulled his chin free. "All right."

Rónán was already up on one knee, the Henry rifle to his shoulder, peering through a gap in the brush toward the treeline above. The militia had not seen them break. The main Irish line still held the attention of the defenders, the exchange of fire heavy and sustained, and the smoke that hung across the slope gave the detachment cover enough.

Rónán fired on the enemy. The lever cycled. He fired again. A third time. He worked the rifle with the same measured rhythm he had shown on the training square, no excitement in it, each shot placed before the trigger was pulled. Three militiamen went down in the treeline in the time it took the others to find their positions in the brush.

"Saints alive," one of the men behind Seamus breathed.

Patch had his rifle up. He found his angle through a gap in the thorn scrub, settled the stock against his shoulder, and held. The barrel steadied. He fired.

The smoke rolled forward and he rose half an inch to see through it.

Seamus seized his arm and hauled him back down into the draw before the brush moved again.

"You don't stand up to look," he said. "Not here."

"Did I hit him?"

"Doesn't matter right now." He pulled Patch's rifle from his hands and performed a rapid reload. "Load and shoot!"

Patch took the rifle. Set his jaw. Nodded once.

The firefight on the slope had found a brutal equilibrium. The Irish line was pushing uphill by degrees, taking losses, the militia holding the treeline, the Gatling gun sweeping whenever the Irish advance thickened. Seamus counted the gun's position from where he knelt. Forty yards up the eastern shoulder, behind a cut log revetment, the crew working it with the practiced ease of men who had received thorough training.

The moment was a question of timing. The gun was traversing back toward the main line, its attention pulled left, the crew focused on the larger target.

"When I go, Rónán covers." He looked at the others. "Patch, you stay on my shoulder. The rest of you, spread out and advance."

Rónán shifted his position without comment, feeding fresh cartridges into the Henry.

Seamus took off, dashing toward the enemy position.

The eastern shoulder gave better ground than the open slope. Rock and root and the broad trunks of pine provided cover every few yards if a man moved between them with intention. Seamus ran fast and low, angling up the hill, Patch a step and a half behind him, and behind them both the crackle of Rónán's cover fire.

The revetment resolved out of the smoke. The loader bent over the hopper, feeding the mechanism with long magazines he pulled from a nearby crate. The gunner worked the crank with his right, traversing back toward the main line, his left steadying the carriage.

Seamus stopped behind a pine trunk. Patch pressed in beside him.

He looked at the boy. Pointed at the loader.

Patch understood. His face went flat and specific, the way Seamus had seen it go on the training square when everything else fell away and there was only the target.

They stepped out together.

Patch's rifle leveled and discharged. The loader folded sideways off the revetment and did not move.

Seamus put his shot through the gunner's shoulder and the man spun off the carriage, the crank swinging free. The gun went silent mid-traverse, its hot barrels pointing at nothing, the mechanical rhythm cut off as abruptly as a clock stopped by hand.

Rónán came in behind them at a run, the Henry empty, a Colt revolver in his right fist. He swept the revetment with three shots. More Irish soldiers were attacking from the flank, catching the British and Canadians off guard.

The silence from the gun lasted only a moment before the rest of the hill noticed.

The Irish line, which had been pressing uphill through the weight of it, found the weight suddenly gone. The advance crested the rise in a wave, and what followed was the close work that no amount of training fully prepares a man for. The bayonets and knives were out, wielded by angry men who had finally closed the distance.

Major Cooke led from the front with sword in hand. When he reached the crest, he used his powerful voice to rally his troops.

"Fág an Bealach!" Clear the way!

The battle cry was repeated by all who knew it. Every veteran of the 69th New York, Seamus included, had heard it a hundred times. The old words inspired courage and action, fueling their assault with renewed motivation.

Seamus drove forward into the treeline, reloading as he moved. Militiamen broke from their positions, some holding, some running, the line fragmenting under the pressure of the Irish assault from front and flank together. He drove his bayonet into a man who turned to face him and felt the resistance and pushed through it the way Cooke had drilled them, through and out the other side.

A shape burst from behind a pine to his left. A British regular, not militia, charged forward with a fixed bayonet and the specific intention of putting it through Seamus's ribs. He had no time. The angle was wrong, his own rifle out of position, the soldier already inside his guard.

Steel rang on steel.

Patch had stepped into the gap between them, his bayonet catching the thrust and turning it, and then driving his own blade forward in one decisive push. The soldier went down hard against the pine trunk and stayed there.

Patch stood over him, breathing through his mouth, his rifle still extended.

Seamus looked at the boy. Patch looked back at him, his face pale, his eyes very wide. A solemn nod of recognition passed between them, and the battle surged on.

The Irish forces, ferocious and numerically superior, drove the combined British and Canadian defenders off of Pine Hill. The assailants, having gained the high ground, used the increased elevation to line up long range rifle fire on their enemies, who were hastily retreating out of range.

Victory came with material rewards. The Ottawa Column

had successfully captured a still functioning Gatling gun with a portion of its ammunition unspent. Other small arms and rations were also recovered. Amongst the loot was a fallen Union Jack.

The Irish soldiers went wild at the sight of the enemy's captured flag. They paraded it around, hoping that British scouts could see what their forces had left behind. Seamus saw it pass by. The Union Jack was spat on, stomped, stretched, torn, and partially burned.

Later that evening, Major Cooke ordered the flag to be preserved. In a final act of symbolic defiance, Irish soldiers posed for a photo featuring the captured colors, their new Gatling gun visible in the background. Seamus, Rónán, and Patch were featured in the center, cracking wry smiles and making provocative gestures.

Under the advice and supervision of Aleksander, Battalion C consolidated their position atop Pine Hill. The Gatling gun was repositioned to face towards Ottawa. New defenses were prepared. Cook fires and tents were permitted for the first time since the beginning of the campaign.

Spirits were running high from the triumph, but the reality of the losses set in when the camp settled down that evening. The assault had cost the column twenty percent of its manpower, wounded and dead.

Father Declan moved amongst the bodies, performing the Rite of Committal.

"Eternal rest grant unto them, O Lord, and let perpetual light shine upon them."

Dr. Cornelius Shaughnessy did his best to establish a rudimentary field hospital. In the light of a dim lantern, the doctor treated gunshot wounds and severe lacerations using a bag of crude medical instruments and only whiskey for the pain.

Seamus was thankful that his boys had only suffered superficial cuts and bruises. He passed his gratitude up to the Lord in a genuine heartfelt prayer later that night.

Major Cooke, having taken account of their current situation, stayed awake late into the night making critical updates to the mission plan. He decided that the column would wait atop Pine Hill, and defend it until additional reinforcements and supplies could be brought in.

At their current location, the column could threaten both Ottawa and Montreal, but they needed the other elements to reach their respective operational checkpoints before the final march on the city could begin. In the meantime, the Battalion C dug in and prepared for the next fight.

9

Tréigean - Betrayal

Twice the British attacked, and twice they were repelled. The Irish position atop Pine Hill had held out for three days, themselves regularly initiating daytime skirmishes and nighttime raids, in a calculated effort to prevent encirclement. The captured weaponry was turned on the redcoats and terrible losses had been inflicted on them.

Seamus, Rónán, and Patch took part in a sneaky, bushwhack blow against an enemy cavalry unit that had moved into the area. Using the element of surprise, the Irish were able to gun down several riders, one of whom was wearing an officer's uniform. A fire was set, and more than twenty horses were set free, scattered to surrounding farmlands.

On the morning of the third day, a Fenian courier reached Pine Hill with fresh reports and messages for Major Cooke. The news was dire. First, Cooke learned that the Montreal Column had stalled in Vermont due to a severe shortage in weapons and ammunition. Promised shipments never arrived. There simply weren't enough rifles to equip all of the volunteers.

The grand invasion plan drawn up by Colonel Sweeny and

the other high-ranking officers of the Fenian Brotherhood was built on the assumption of twenty thousand soldiers crossing into Canada. As it played out, fewer than ten percent of that number had materialized. The transport corridor had not been closed and the enemy had moved reinforcements into the region by rail. Additionally, Canadians were mustering in droves to fight with the militias.

The logistical failure of the Montreal Column fundamentally changed the viability of the entire operation. Major Cooke knew this. His mind ran calculations, all outcomes inevitably dire.

The courier had more to share. Uncle Sam had officially weighed in and withdrawn any supposed support for the Irish cause. Prior to the invasion, the Fenian Brotherhood had many fraternal connections to high-ranking officers of the US military, members of Congress including both the House and the Senate, as well as Governors and state legislators all across the northern United States. These connections had been vectors for volunteers, funding, as well as weapons and munitions.

This open sympathy for Irish nationalism was largely tolerated for a number of reasons. Primarily, it was because Irish-Americans represented a powerful voting bloc in many cities and states across the Union, strong enough to topple established politicians at every level. Second to that, many former members of the Lincoln Administration had not overlooked the fact that England had flirted with recognition of the Confederacy. This meddling in America's affairs crossed a line, and for some, stripping Ireland from the British Empire seemed like an appropriate response.

In the first week of June, US President Andrew Johnson, under diplomatic pressure from London and her vassals, issued his 'Neutrality Proclamation'. It was far from neutral, amounting to an outright betrayal of the Irish cause and prior commitments. Federal troops were deployed to New York under the command of none other than General Ulysses S Grant.

"No!" Cooke had shouted when he read the name. "You bastard! How could you?"

A generation of Irish-American immigrants had served under Grant and won him many of his most crucial victories. Without their sacrifice, it may well have been Grant who signed surrender documents at Appomattox.

Major Cooke read on. The Feds had begun seizing Fenian arms shipments and stockpiles. No additional reinforcements or supplies were coming, he knew at once. The Feds had even begun arresting Fenian leaders, including Colonel Sweeny, who was taken into custody shortly after the operation launched.

Similar anti-Fenian crackdowns were underway in British-occupied Ireland and Australia. The entire organization was being systematically dismantled. Harsh punishments were being doled out to dissuade any more rebel activity.

The last bit of the courier's message alluded to suspicions that British spies had infiltrated the movement weeks ago, and that internal sabotage contributed to the operation's discovery and eventual failure.

Major Cooke went red. He cursed. He swore. He kicked a metal bucket clear off the hill. Dejected, he let the news spread throughout the camp. The men received the updates and an immediate depression fell over them.

They would not capture Ottawa, and they would not free Ireland.

That night, Cooke met with the other leaders of the column.

They had a long, difficult discussion about defense, retreat, and surrender. After some argument, they reached a sober conclusion.

At the midnight hour, a portion of deserters fled from the camp, leaving their weapons behind and sneaking off to the south. Guards reported the incident, and a harsh response was considered. Cooke ultimately decided to let them go. He told the remaining men that if anyone else wished to flee, that they best go now as well.

* * *

The morning came in grey and still, the mist sitting low across the slope, softening the treeline into shapes without edges. Seamus crouched behind a pine log at the forward perimeter and watched the open ground below the hill.

The rider appeared out of the mist at a walk.

A white horse, the color of him almost luminous in the grey light, moving up the slope with the unhurried confidence of an animal that had never been shot at. The rider sat straight in the saddle, one hand loose on the reins. Two redcoats flanked him at a distance, their rifles slung, their faces forward.

"Seamus." Patch's voice, low and tight.

He didn't look at the boy. He watched the horse.

"I see them."

Patch had his rifle across the log, his cheek already against the stock, the barrel tracking the lead rider with the slow patience of a cat watching something it intended to catch.

"Hold fire," Seamus said.

"He's within range."

"I know he is. Hold fire."

The white cloth flying above them caught a breath of air and opened briefly, then collapsed again against the pole. The rider made no gesture of urgency, no sign that he understood or cared that a dozen rifles were fixed on his chest. He simply rode uphill at the same easy walk, as though arriving at a social engagement he had been mildly inconvenienced to attend.

Word passed back through the perimeter. Men appeared along the defensive line, some still chewing their morning ration. Liam Cooke materialized from the command tent behind the crest and stood with his arms crossed, watching the approach without moving to meet it.

The British officer halted at the edge of the camp and looked down from the saddle at the assembled Irishmen with the expression of a man examining goods at a market stall and finding the display roughly as expected.

He was young. Younger than Seamus had anticipated, thirty at most, perhaps less, clean-shaven where every other man on this hill wore a week of campaign growth at minimum. Even Patch had some fuzz cropping up on his jaw. The British officer's uniform was immaculate in a way that suggested a man who had not been anywhere near the fighting. Fine leather gloves covered his small hands.

He waited.

Cooke let him wait.

A full minute passed. The horse shifted its weight. The officer did not shift his.

Rónán appeared at Seamus's shoulder and looked the rider over with the measuring eye of a man pricing livestock. "Christ, look at the cut of him. Noble prick, thinks he has magic in his blood, I bet."

Cooke walked forward from the crest. He stopped at the log line and looked up at the rider with a flat, patient expression.

The officer straightened in the saddle.

"I am Captain Edward Ashworth Pelham." He produced each word with the deliberate enunciation of a man who expected his name to carry weight on contact. "His Majesty's Sixteenth Regiment of Foot, seconded to the Eastern District garrison command, acting under the authority of—"

"Get on with it," Cooke said.

Pelham paused. He looked at Cooke as if he were a dog who had just addressed him. Then he continued.

"—acting under the authority of Brigadier General Napier, commanding His Majesty's forces in the Ottawa district." He reached into his coat and produced a folded document, which he held out at arm's length. One of the flanking redcoats walked his horse forward to take it, crossed to the log line, and held it out to Cooke.

Cooke did not take it.

The redcoat held it a moment longer, then withdrew.

"My message is brief." Pelham folded the document back into his coat as though returning it to safekeeping. "Lay down your arms immediately. Submit to arrest. And you shall be tried and sentenced fairly by the law of the Crown." He let a beat pass. "Refuse, and face annihilation."

The word landed on the hilltop and sat there.

Behind Seamus, no one moved. No one spoke. The mist drifted between the pines and the white horse stood entirely still, as though it too was waiting for the answer.

The prevailing consensus among the Irish was that surrender would mean being taken before a colonial magistrate for a brief procedural show, and then a prompt hanging. Retreat was likewise a doomed suggestion. The column would never make it back to the Saint Lawrence.

They were going to fight. That was their only option, to plant their heels in the dirt, to shoulder their rifles, and to fight and die beneath the Irish flag. They resolved to do just that, drawing upon their faith in the Christian God and their shared ancestral strength of the ancient Gaels. Courage filled their bellies where food did not.

Terms rejected, Captain Pelham smirked. He started to turn his horse about and depart, but something in him couldn't go without saying something more.

"Many of us were hoping for this result," Pelham said, his voice dripping with contempt and morbid satisfaction. "Your foolish decision to desecrate the Union Jack will come at a terrible cost which we intend to collect from your flesh. You are surrounded. You are outnumbered and outgunned. And soon... you'll all be dead."

With the final words exchanged, the English riders returned to their lines. With days of preparation, thousands of British and Canadian troops had assembled in the area. There were line infantry units that stretched across the entire battlefield. Cavalry maneuvered around the edges and in the rear. Multiple batteries of field cannon were arrayed against Pine Hill, their heavy barrels turned upward at a slight angle, catching the morning sun as it broke through the clouds.

Father Declan hurried amongst the Irish infantry, saying quick prayers and blessings. When he reached Seamus, Rónán, and Patch he said to them, "Keep the Lord in your heart and you'll have nothing to fear." The young men bowed their heads and prepared themselves.

The first shell came within the hour. It landed short, forty yards below the Irish line, and threw a column of black earth twenty feet into the air.

Seamus pressed flat against the log revetment. The sound arrived a half-second after the impact, a concussive crack that compressed the air against his eardrums and left a high ringing in its wake. Dirt and splinters of pine rained down across his back.

The second shell did not land short.

It came in over the crest and detonated inside the treeline, and the white pine it hit simply ceased to be a tree and became a hundred spinning fragments of wood, each one moving at a velocity that made no distinction between bark and bone. Two men from A Company went down in the same instant, folded into the ground by the blast wave before the debris had finished falling.

"Down!" Cooke's voice carried across the hilltop over the ringing.

There was nowhere further down to go. Seamus already had his face against the log, his rifle pulled under him. Around him the Irish line had compressed itself into whatever the earth offered — depressions, root systems, the shallow trenches Aleksander had pushed them to dig two days prior.

The barrage found its rhythm. Not random. Methodical. The British gunners walked their fire across the hilltop in overlapping lines, each battery finding its arc and repeating it, adjusting by degrees, the way a man sweeps a room with a lantern. The ground shook in a sustained, rolling percussion that made thinking difficult and movement worse.

A shell came down on the surgery tent.

Seamus saw it happen. He had turned his head to check Patch's position when the round struck the canvas structure sixty yards behind the crest, and the tent folded inward around the detonation point and then outward in the same instant, the whole structure lifting off the ground before collapsing into a burning heap of canvas and shattered timber. In a flash, Dr. Shaughnessy's practice was ended.

"They're moving!" The shout came from the forward perimeter. "Infantry advancing!"

Seamus rose to one knee behind the log and looked down the slope through the haze. The British line came up out of the mist in good order — red coats dressed into columns, officers on horseback moving along the flanks, the pace deliberate and unhurried. Behind them the cannon continued to fire, the shells passing overhead now with a sound like tearing paper, plunging into the treeline at the crest.

"Gatling!" Cooke shouted.

The captured gun swung to meet them. The crew had it traversing before the order finished, and when the crank turned, the sound was everything Seamus remembered from the first assault on this hill — that continuous mechanical beat, indifferent to the men it found. The British advance broke across it. The front rank folded. The second pushed through the gaps left by the first and continued uphill, and the gun swept back across them, and more went down, and still they came.

The ammunition ran dry in under three minutes.

The crew cranked twice on an empty mechanism and the sound died. They abandoned the gun under a volley that stripped bark from the pine beside it, running low and fast to the rear, leaving the Gatling cooling on its carriage.

"Rifles!" Cooke's voice. "Fire at will!"

Seamus found his position behind the log and began to shoot. Load, aim, fire. The drill from Delaware County, reduced to its essentials. The slope was thick with movement and smoke. He picked targets where he could see them clearly and did not think about what came between the trigger pull and the impact. Patch was two feet to his right, firing steadily, his face a mask of rigid concentration. Rónán worked the lever-action Henry, adjusting its sights for long range. He punished the reckless officers with accurate shots that had zero respect for their rank or titles.

Cooke was on his feet twenty yards back from the log line, his Colt in his right hand. He shot a redcoat who crested the perimeter in the face and then shot another who came in behind the first, and then drew his sword with the empty revolver still in his fist and stood there in the open with the blade at his side, watching the slope, beckoning the English to come and meet their end.

The grenadiers came with the second wave.

Seamus heard them before he understood what he was hearing. It was a different sound beneath the rifle fire, a shorter, rounder detonation, not the sharp crack of a bullet impact or the heavy boom of cannons, but something that began with a burning sizzle and then a loud pop. The trench line was degrading rapidly.

"Grenades!" Rónán shouted. "Grenades!"

Men broke from the perimeter, running back through the trees. Not cowardice. The math of the thing, the same calculation every soldier made when the ground itself went into retreat. Seamus held his position and kept shooting.

Then the lit grenade landed.

It came in from the right and struck the base of the log directly in front of Patch, the fuse already short, a finger's length of burning cord left between the present moment and what came next.

Seamus did not think. He grabbed Patch by the collar of his jacket with both hands and hauled him backward off the log with everything he had.

A bright flash blinded him temporarily.

He came back to himself on his side in the dirt. His ears produced only a high, clean tone, unbroken. Patch was beside him, already pushing up onto his hands and knees, his face grey with displaced earth. His rifle was lost in the chaos.

Seamus got his hands under himself and pushed upright. The log revetment was gone. Splinters and turned earth where it had been. The smoke was everywhere now, thick and acrid, burning the back of his throat.

Behind them the Irish line had collapsed inward from the forward perimeter, men falling back through the pines toward the southern crest. Cooke was still visible through the smoke, sword drawn, moving between the trees, battling British infantry at close quarters.

Major Cooke cut down two men in rapid succession, cleaving their torsos into uneven portions with his heavy broadsword. But the enemy were too many. A squad of redcoats closed on him and their bayonets found his heart.

Seamus did not have time to weep. He grabbed Patch's arm and pulled him upright.

"Move." He got his shoulder under the boy and drove him south through the trees, away from the forward line, toward the southern edge of the hill where the slope fell away into the open field below. Patch's legs found their rhythm after three steps and he ran on his own.

Seamus looked back towards the camp. The Irish had been routed. The pine cathedral that once sheltered the hilltop had been destroyed by cannon fire.

Father Declan, too old to run, was surrounded by enemies. The Canadians did not slay him however, having recognized him as a noncombatant. He surrendered and was taken away at gunpoint.

Nearby, Rónán continued to fight, drawing the enemy's attention away from Seamus and Patch temporarily.

"We have to run," Seamus told the boy.

"No. We have to fight—"

"The fight is over, lad. We lost."

A tear threatened to emerge on Seamus's cheek, but he was too dehydrated for it to spawn. "South. We'll lose them in the bogs. But we have to go. NOW!"

Seamus, Patch, and a half dozen other soldiers broke from the camp at Pine Hill and routed from the battlefield. Rónán too was forced to withdraw when he expended his last rifle cartridge. He did not follow the others however, instead striking off to the east.

The British and the Canadians pursued the remaining survivors of the Ottawa Column with cavalry. Many men were ridden down, dispatched by sabers and hooves.

Seamus and Patch ran for their lives. Ragged and near exhaustion, they reached the bog that the column they had passed through in the week prior. Reluctantly, they began to negotiate their way through the mud, hoping to lose their pursuers in the rough terrain.

Progress was slow and difficult, as it had been before. The swamp was unfamiliar and hostile to them, as if it knew they were invaders. Patch lost a boot, pulled off by the incessant sucking of the wet soils under their weight. He stopped to try and retrieve it.

Dragoons appeared at the edge of the bog. They spotted Seamus and Patch and wasted no time taking aim with their carbines. Shots rang out. A bullet tore through the abdomen of Patch, punching a big red hole in the boy's body.

Seamus saw it happen and knew at once what it meant.

"No! Dammit, no!"

Gutshot, Patch began to bleed uncontrollably. He couldn't resist it, and moments later, death claimed him there in the bog.

In a terrible fit of grief, Seamus left Patch where he lay, slowly sinking into the muddy waters. Seamus closed his eyes, gritted his teeth, and waded deeper into the swamps. The British let off a few more shots, but did not follow him.

10

Dícheall - Endeavor

The bog was as cruel and indifferent as ever.

Seamus's boots filled on the third step and stayed full, the cold water rising to his thighs, then his waist, the mud below yielding and then gripping with each forward push. He moved through it for what felt like hours, until the riders' voices faded behind him and the only sound was the water and his own ragged breathing and the occasional crack of a branch somewhere in the spruce above.

He made the treeline before dark. He slept in the roots of a fallen birch, curled into the hollow beneath the upended root ball, his wet clothes plastered to him. He did not dream. There was nothing left in him to dream with.

He walked south for three days.

A farmhouse on the second morning had a hayloft he found before the family stirred, and he lay in the straw and slept again, waking to the sound of chickens and a child's voice below and the smell of woodsmoke from the house, and he lay still and stared at the roof boards until the farm went quiet and then he slipped back out before the sun was fully up, but not before pilfering a few chicken eggs.

He found the river by sound before he saw it. The Saint Lawrence was high and fast, the current visible as dark wrinkles on the grey surface, and he stood on the bank for a long moment and looked at the American side. The Land of Freedom was within reach. He stepped into the water.

The cold hit him like a blow across the chest, driving the air out, and he went under once before he found his stroke and surfaced. The current took him sideways and he fought across it rather than against it, angling downstream, his arms pulling long and mechanical. His boots dragged. At the midpoint his legs stopped cooperating properly and he swam on his arms alone, his chin barely above the waterline, the far bank pulling closer by increments that felt minuscule.

He crawled out on the south bank on his hands and knees and sat in the mud with his chest heaving until his breathing became something he could control again.

He walked toward Potsdam with his wet boots squelching and his coat hanging heavy off his shoulders and his hands open at his sides. The morning light sat pale and cold on the empty road. A crow watched him from a fence post and flew off without alarm.

They came out from both sides of the road simultaneously.

Four of them. Civilian clothes, Federal Marshal badges, rifles up and levelled before he had processed that they were men and not shadows. The one at the center, heavyset, with a reddish moustache, had a Colt Army pistol pointed at Seamus's chest.

"Stop where you are."

Seamus stopped.

He looked at the guns. He looked at his own hands, pale and empty, the knuckles still raw from the fighting, the river water still dripping from his cuffs. His legs had nothing left in them. The bog had taken his reserve and the river had taken whatever remained.

He raised his hands.

The marshal with the moustache moved forward, his eyes reading Seamus the way a man reads a terrain map, looking for hidden features.

"Fenian Brotherhood." He said it like a charge, without inflection. "You are under arrest by the authority of the United States Federal Marshals Service, acting under Presidential Proclamation."

Nobody spoke.

The marshal holstered the Colt and stepped forward, and cold iron closed around Seamus's wrists. They took him to a holding station, and then to jail.

Seamus, alongside other Fenians, was brought before a judge. He was an old New Yorker who had no sympathy for the Irish rebels. His court wasted no time finding Seamus and the other men guilty of violating the Neutrality Proclamation, waging war on a peaceful nation, insurrection, and treason. Additionally, the prosecution cited an incident in which some Fenian men on the run engaged in a gun battle with the US Marshals. Seamus had no involvement, but was assigned blame nonetheless, adding more charges to the list.

Seamus was sentenced to life in prison, which was actually a small form of mercy. The prosecutors had pushed for the death penalty, but the judge thought better of it. He did not wish to make any of the captured Fenians into martyrs for the cause. He'd rather quietly erase their story with a long, boring sentence.

Seamus was transferred to Auburn prison.

By 1867, Auburn Prison had become one of the most brutal institutions in American history. The prison administration had developed a program of absolute control. The system required prisoners to work during the day in groups and be kept in solitary confinement at night, with enforced silence at all times. Absolute silence at work, in the yard, in the cells, at meals. The Prisoners marched in unison in lockstep formation, arms locked to the convict in front, required to look to one side, forbidden from looking at guards or other inmates. No letters. No visitors.

A system of bells controlled the prisoners. It told them when to wake, when to work, when to sleep.

A single iron clang from somewhere above the cellblock, resonating down through the stone floors and into his bones before his mind had fully separated from sleep. Seamus was upright and dressed before the echo died. That was the rule. That was the only rule, repeated endlessly in its variations: be upright, be dressed, be silent, be still, be nothing that required acknowledgment from another human being.

The cell was six feet by eight. A plank bed, a bucket. The conditions were stark, offering zero comfort of any kind.

The door opened. He stepped out into the corridor and found his place in the line without looking at the man ahead of him. He locked his left arm over the man's right, felt the answering grip settle into place, and looked to his left as instructed. Not at the guard. Not at the man ahead. At the stone wall moving past him as the lockstep carried the line forward, each man's feet finding the cadence from the man in front, the rhythm transmitted body to body down the entire column like a current through wire.

His head was shaved. Had been shaved on the first day, a

guard moving a razor across his scalp with the bored efficiency of a man stripping bark. The stripes of his uniform were coarse wool, grey and black, and they itched at the collar. He had stopped noticing the itch somewhere in the second week.

The dining hall held two hundred men on long benches, their backs straight, their eyes forward, their spoons moving from bowl to mouth in a silence so complete it had texture. Seamus ate his porridge. It was thin, salt-heavy. He kept his eyes on the table in front of him.

Across the hall, not thirty feet distant, a man sat whose face he knew. Seamus had recognized him on the third day. A Brotherhood man, older, from one of the Brooklyn circles. He had been at the Oimelc Festival, had stood near the stage when the speakers took the platform, had sung along to the verses with his hat held to his chest. His name was Cormac something. They had never spoken directly.

They could not speak now.

Seamus looked at his porridge. Cormac looked at his porridge. Between them, the enforced silence pressed down on the room like a physical weight.

He had spotted others. Four Fenians in total that he could identify with certainty, possibly a fifth whose profile was familiar but whose name he could not place. They moved through the same routines he moved through, locked into the same lockstep, eating from the same bowls, sleeping behind the same iron doors. They passed within arm's reach of each other in the corridors sometimes, arms locked to strangers, eyes directed to the left, and did not speak and did not signal and did not nod.

The workroom was on the east wing, a long rectangular space with high windows that let in pale columns of light through thick glass. He wove shoes. Had been doing so since his first week, a task assigned without explanation and never varied. The wooden base, the leather upper, the waxed thread, the curved needle. His hands performed the sequence independent of his mind within a fortnight. They did it now while the rest of him sat somewhere apart and watched.

There was noise in the room. Two hundred men working with their hands produced considerable sound, thread pulling through leather, the knock of a last against a bench, the rhythm of the stitching irons, but no human sound. No voice. No cough that was not immediately suppressed. No scrape of a stool that was not made as small as possible.

A man three benches ahead of him dropped a tool on the stone floor.

The guard was there in four steps. The correction was administered with mean leather, quick and precise, over the shoulders of the crouching man. Nobody looked. Nobody flinched visibly. Seamus watched his own hands and continued making shoes.

He understood the system. He had understood it within days of his arrival. The silence was not incidental. The lockstep was not merely practical. Strip a man of his voice and you strip him of his people, because solidarity requires communication and communication requires speech and speech requires the acknowledgment that you exist as a person worth addressing. Deny a man that, and he becomes isolated not merely from others but from himself.

The British did it in Ireland, on a societal scale. The language suppressed. The songs banned. The gatherings prohibited. The slow, administrative erasure of the means by which people become a people rather than a collection of mouths requiring management.

Auburn had refined it into a rigid order.

The bell rang at midday. He stood, locked his arm into the line, and walked.

The yard was a rectangle of packed earth enclosed by walls. The men walked it in a circuit, the lockstep maintained, eyes left. The sky above the walls was a flat winter grey, and the cold came off the stone in waves.

It was a terrible, miserable existence. Seamus wallowed in pity, depression, and despair for months, bottling all of his emotions up deep inside his chest, unable to express anything.

After six months of imprisonment, a small glimmer of hope was able to break through the prison walls. Someone spoke to Seamus. A whisper in the night. A sympathetic guard, himself half-Irish, had taken to passing messages to the interned Fenians.

The guard would visit Seamus's cell in late hours of night, pausing at the door just long enough to pass along a few sentences. He told Seamus that popular rallies had been organized in the US, Ireland, and the UK, demanding fair treatment for the Fenians, who were being referred to as political prisoners and prisoners of war.

This news lit a spark for Seamus, something like hope. Each night, he waited desperately for the guard to come and whisper updates to him. They rarely came; more often than not, the guard neglected to visit.

On one cold December night, the guard brought Seamus troubling news. In hushed words, the guard told a story of a bomb plot. Irish operatives, in an attempt to free their comrades within, had detonated a large explosive device near Clerkenwell Prison. The blast damaged nearby houses, killed a dozen people and injured more than one hundred. No prisoners escaped.

The guard did not speak to Seamus again for months. The bits he'd let slip were insignificant and only served to dampen his low spirits. However, Seamus had gotten it in his mind that the prisoners at Auburn should stage a revolt. He beseeched the sympathetic guard to help him organize with the other Fenians on the inside. The guard refused, simply walking away whenever Seamus started his inquiry.

Years went by. Seamus rose, worked, ate, and slept. His life being an unending sequence of rigid routines, enforced by the violence of the prison guards, who flogged him more than once for violating their rules.

The only updates that reached Seamus were of failure, delay, and setback. The remaining Fenian circles had regrouped and formed secondary organizations in the US and Australia, and continued to operate in England as well. They had made several more attempts to free their men in captivity. Most had failed, although Seamus did hear about a prisoner transfer wagon that was intercepted.

During the long hours of the day, Seamus's mind would retreat into memories. He thought of Mayo. He thought of Manhattan. He thought of fresh bread and strong drinks he missed. He thought of the ladies he'd been fortunate enough to know, and wondered where they might be now. He thought of his brothers and fallen comrades. He thought of Major Cooke and his last stand, but chased away the memory of young Patch bleeding to death in the bog.

Seamus often thought of Rónán, his closest friend and ally. When he saw him last, Rónán was executing a fighting withdrawal. Seamus hoped and prayed that Rónán had survived the battle of Pine Hill. Had he made it out? Was he also captured? Or was he free? Seamus had no answers for these questions.

After months of silence, a fresh report reached Seamus. Irish prisoner James Wilson had secretly sent a letter to New York City journalist John Devoy, who joined the effort to rescue the Irish political prisoners. Using donations collected by Devoy from Irish-Americans, Fenian escapee John Boyle O'Reilly, then living in Boston, purchased a merchant ship and sailed her to international waters off Rockingham, Western Australia. From there, they organized the clandestine escape of six Fenian prisoners, spiriting them away from the British Penal Colony.

Seamus had been delighted to hear this story. He pictured every whispered word and a vivid image appeared in his mind. Seamus was envious of those who were rescued, knowing that their torment was brought to an end. He allowed himself to dream of freedom and of a second chance at life beyond the walls of Auburn prison.

The guard had shared his joy and agreed that a similar effort was likely underway to free Seamus and the other Fenians imprisoned there, but he had no specific details to offer.

The guard stopped coming on a Tuesday.

Seamus knew the day only because the workroom received a delivery of new leather stock on Tuesdays, and he had been marking the weeks by that small variation in the otherwise featureless rhythm of the place. The man simply did not appear at the cell door that night. Nor the next night. Nor the one after that.

A month passed. Then two. Seamus lay in his cell through the long silent nights and listened for footsteps that did not come, and eventually he stopped listening.

Reassigned, possibly. Dismissed. He had no way of knowing,

and knowing would have changed nothing. The man was gone and the dark was complete again, and Seamus turned onto his side on the plank bed and stared at the wall until the bell told him to rise.

The years accumulated the way silt accumulates — invisibly, without event, each layer indistinguishable from the one beneath it. The bell. The lockstep. The workroom. The yard. The cell. The bell again. Seamus's hands grew calloused in the specific topography of shoe work, the thread grooves cutting permanent channels into his fingertips, the curved needle leaving a small raised scar on the pad of his right thumb that he could feel in the dark when there was nothing else to do with his hands.

The guards flogged him still, for violations both real and perceived. He took the leather across his shoulders and said nothing, because there was nothing to say and no one to say it to, and afterward he walked back to his place in the lockstep and looked to the left as instructed.

His body moved through the days with a completeness that his mind no longer matched. He woke. He dressed. He marched. He worked. He ate. He slept. The body had become fluent in Auburn's grammar and ran through its conjugations without assistance, leaving the mind free to go wherever minds go when they have been systematically deprived of anything worth thinking about.

Which was the problem. The mind went, but it did not always return cleanly.

There had been a guard. He was certain of that much. He had stood at the cell door and whispered things. Seamus had heard them. Or believed he had heard them. The rallies, the political prisoners, the rescue ship off the coast of Australia.

He turned these memories in his hands like a man examining coins of uncertain provenance, trying to assess their weight against the known world. The harder he looked at them, the less solid they became. Details softened at the edges. The guard's face went generic, then vague, then absent entirely. The words he had whispered rearranged themselves slightly each time Seamus reached for them, the way a sentence changes meaning when you are not certain you have remembered it correctly.

Had any of it happened? Or had he lain on the plank bed in the small hours, cold and alone and desperate enough, and built the whole architecture of it out of want and desperation?

He could not say. He genuinely could not say.

The not-knowing was its own particular weight, separate from the rest. A man could endure known suffering. He could measure it, name it, set it against whatever he believed in and find some equilibrium. But he could not stand on ground he was no longer sure existed.

He stopped reaching for the memories. Let them sit wherever they had gone, neither claimed nor discarded.

He wove his shoes. He walked his circuit. He ate his porridge and looked at his bowl and placed one foot in front of the other in the lockstep, his arm locked over the arm of a man whose name he did not know and to whom he would never speak, and the days moved through him the way the lockstep moved through the corridor, forward, rhythmic, indifferent to where it was going.

His bottled up emotions solidified into a lasting source of bitterness towards the Crown, towards the US Government, towards tyranny and authority of every kind.

Amnesty arrived on March 1st, 1877. As one of his final acts as President, Ulysses S. Grant issued a Presidential Pardon for the remaining Fenian prisoners at Auburn. This decision was not made out of kindness or recognition of the injustice that had been dealt upon the Irish. Instead, it was the discrete solution to a sensitive political situation that had taken on an international character.

As the papers told it, a prominent British consular official was kidnapped while visiting New York City. His captors were the remnants of Fenian circle headed by none other than Seamus's closest friend, Rónán. They took the British official hostage, not to harm him, but to hold him publicly and demand the Fenian prisoners' release. They treated him correctly, fed him well, and made their demands through the press.

The British government could not stand to be seen negotiating with kidnappers. The American government could not permit British diplomatic personnel to be held by Irish rebels. The political pressure converged from both sides simultaneously. A deal was quietly made through back channels. The consular official was to be released, and the Fenian prisoners amnestied.

After being subjected to harsh, inhumane conditions for more than a decade, Seamus was finally set free. His hastily written pardon, bearing the signature of the US President, represented a political concession. A small one, but one that made all the difference to the men who had been liberated.

Seamus was unceremoniously plucked from the prison population, alongside a handful of others, and processed out of the system.

His brothers were waiting for him on the outside, ready to welcome him back into the world. Rónán was among them.

Surrounded by friends and loved ones, once again the recipient of compassion, support, and mutual respect, Seamus felt his humanity return to him. What the Auburn system had tried to extinguish in him was instead renewed.

"What's next?" Rónán asked him. "Manhattan? Mayo?"

Seamus turned his face up toward the sun and let the light shine on him.

"Only the Lord knows."

www.ingramcontent.com/pod-product-compliance
Lightning Source LLC
LaVergne TN
LVHW090614110826
845146LV00001B/390

9798998671340